I0638966

Preserved   Intellect
Agglomeration

Milton J Southerland

"Suppose it was so, that we not only observe the virtual world but are, in fact, a part of one."

Also included in this book, by the same author:

Harvest 2050AD
Starting on Page 147
The saddest book I ever wrote.

**Milton J Southerland
2441 Old Hwy 411 South
Chatsworth, Georgia 30705 USA**

Voice in the Garden

ISBN: 978-0-578-02091-4

For my wife

Louise

The players:

Doctor Frank who started the original brain preservation program.
Doctor Ann Stein his assistant.
Doctor Trey Banks Supervisor on another level.
Jon the kid computer hacker.
Mike assistant to Doctor Stein
David assistant to Doctor Banks
Rev Dewey Wright a preacher in Doctor Frank's world.
Senator Crouch approves the program, at least in his mind.
Ben is a farmer and is from the outside.
Hannah is Ben's sweetheart.
Brad is in Ben's world.
Sam emerges into Ben's world.
Pierre is Ann's last chess opponent.
Bizmortee is the last United States President

Introduction

How does one use his mind to examine itself?
Objectivity is obviously the first casualty. We might
consider that we have reached the limits of knowledge
while actually only reaching our limits. For example, a
gallon jug, if filled to the brim with water, might think that it
holds all the water there is in existence. Even while
submerged in a tub of water, it might assume that what exist
inside itself is all that there is. Of course a jug cannot think or
reason, as humans, we have that distinct advantage over our
vast surroundings. We can reason and come to conclusions
based on the information we gather. A wise man knows that if
he reaches into his deepest self and out to the vastness of the
universe, still he is but a jug, a container with limits, with a
measure of knowledge surrounded by that which he does not
know. Is it real or is it illusion? The mind must decide. But
that does not change whether it is one or the other.

Our very well-being is determined by the actions of
people who believe *their* knowledge is superior.

*"Inside our minds we journey in a
world that is often quite different from reality."*

A futuristic story.

Chapter One

The majestic halls of Congress have echoed with the sounds of debate for hundreds of years now. Today is no different. The, seemingly, endless oratory, the maddening debates go on and on. Now word processors soundlessly, except for the slight clatter of fingers on the keyboard, are used to type and retype would-be law. Cut and paste is a must, to make the stream of changes coming from the Senate floor and the committee chambers. A secret phone call could change the meaning of a page with the insertion or deletion of a single word. Such were the games played on Capitol Hill. It was not uncommon for an elected official to vote for a bill only to find out later that it meant nothing like what he had intended. It would be too embarrassing for him to admit that, so he says nothing.

"They're dead." Senator Crouch bellowed. He was tall and silver-headed atop a bulky frame. He was standing now and leaning as far as he dared over the table in front of him toward his adversary across the room. His opponent was of slight build and looked up at the giant across the room. He did not rise or raise his voice.

"They're very much alive." He replied in a calm almost apologetic tone, which quieted the big man across the way for a moment. How do you argue with a man who won't raise his voice?

"They're rows of brains on a shelf!" Crouch replied.

"I beg to differ with your assumption. True they appear to be only brains on a shelf. Although you did not use the word 'only', it was implied by your tone. They, in fact, live their lives as they see fit." The slight built man was the director of a secret project called PI for short. It meant Preserved Intellect. His name was Doctor Frank. As a matter-of-fact, he could have strung a half dozen 'PhDs' to his name.

"Doctor Frank. They're dead and do not know it."
The Senator said from a seated position.

"How do we know, Senator? We cannot decide when life starts. How can we know when it ends?"

"Their body is gone. Their soul is gone. They're in a glass bubble. They're ..."

"Is the soul gone? Where does the soul reside?" Doctor Frank took off his glasses and peered at the Senator across the room. The Senator looked from one colleague to another and then behind him at his assistant.

"Alright. Alright. You will get your funding." The big man said with a sigh. He knew he could not stop the funding. It had been untouchable for years but still he must appear to be looking out for the interest of the overburdened taxpayer. Doctor Frank ventured a smile in the Senator's direction then around the room.

"Thank you ladies and gentlemen. Now, if you will excuse me, I have a lot of work to do." Doctor Frank gathered his documents into an untidy pile and left the room with his assistant, who occasionally stooped to retrieve some paper the doctor had dropped. It was a little game he played. He knew he dropped them. His assistant knew, he knew, that he dropped them. Neither ever mentioned their knowledge. Doctor Frank actually like the glimpses he got of his pretty assistant picking up his papers. Her hair always fell over her face and she would push it back behind her ears only to have to bend to pick up another paper causing her hair to fall again. It was not nice of him to play this game but it amused him. She had been with him for years, actually, since her college days. He doubted if she minded too very much.

The lab techs watched the monitors with amusement. Each and every action of the brains gave off a signal, most of which, they recognized. There were still some unknowns though. Anomalous events still to be explained. The human brain was indeed a mystery and they were silently thankful that it was so. The industry had made way for a nice future for them. The many labs scattered across the world had improved the lives of many young geniuses. It was decided that there would be many labs rather than one huge project for many reasons. One reason, of course, and the public reason, was so the whole world could benefit from the financial gains to be offered. The main scientific reason was so the brains could be kept in a location near their original home and place of employment to make the input of data easier. It was a primary goal of the project to maintain the continuity of the brain's life. Keeping them in their local culture did much to accomplish that goal. Much care was taken to make the transition from living being to the brain container as non-traumatic as possible.

The events of whatever incident caused the death or non-usability of the body were carefully altered, in the memory of the brain, to eliminate death and replace it with a slow recovery. During the slow recovery there was enough unconsciousness to allow for the change-over and to input the proper programming to bridge the gap between life in a human body and life in a glass lab container. So far, the brains had simply continued the life they had already been living. There were few indications of stress or panic. True. It had been necessary to terminate some brains along the way.

Watching the many monitors was like speed reading a bunch of novels all at once. The techs watched through the joy and tragedy of many lives. The data feeds going into the brains were an astounding array of scenarios of personal life and world events. Although world events were constant for all the brains, the personal scenarios were seemingly endless. Those were taken from real lives merged with the lives of the survivors of the brain donor. It was a complicated algorithm understood fully, only by the author, Doctor

Frank.

The phone beeped and was answered by one of the techs. It was Doctor Frank's assistant on the phone.

"There has been a terrible accident! Doctor Frank was killed! He is on life support but the medical doctors are saying there is too much damage to his body for him to live. Send a team at once to retrieve his brain. His knowledge is much to valuable to loose." She hung up the phone and wept.

Ann Stein had been assisting Doctor Frank for many years. She still looked the young post-graduate student except for her demeanor of self-confidence which demanded attention from others in whatever room she was in. Now, she was standing beside the tech's station who was in charge of monitoring Doctor Frank's brain.

"See." The tech started. "The brain is lighting up the screen with activity. We will filter off any new discoveries it comes up with."

At this point she moved one hand only slightly. It was enough to quiet the tech. She watched the data flash across the screen. To most people, it was a screen full of gobblegook, but to the tech it was a steady stream of information as he instantly converted the images to a play of human activity.

"It is not just a brain, Mike." Doctor Stein told him. A tear escaped her left eye. She wiped it away and as she looked at it on her finger finished her thought.

"I want him referred to as Doctor Frank. He deserves more respect than 'it'."

"Of course Doctor. I'm sorry." Mike said apologetically.

"That's alright Mike. Just doing your job."

"Doctor Stein?"

"Yes Mike." She gave him a portion of her attention as she watched the screen. She was capable of dividing her attention and still function perfectly on at least two levels.

"You and Doctor Frank were close?" Mike inquired.

"We were as close as any twins. He said I understood his thoughts. He was much more intelligent than me though. I did understand his pattern of thought. We were bonded on the mental level in a way that few will ever experience. Yes.

We were close."

An uncomfortable silence followed during which the tech again became the subordinate. She had unconsciously placed her hand on Mike's shoulder. Mike was very perceptive in his own right. He realized that, for a moment he was a conduit between the two doctors.

The mind is very powerful. Mike felt the strength of two very strong minds reaching for each other. Searching across two worlds. Ann was no longer in the world Doctor Frank lived in. In his world it was Ann who met with tragedy. He must go on. Looking at the screen Ann felt his pain, his emptiness and the pain was too real.

She straightened her pink suit and clicked her heels as she assumed the posture of authority once more. Starting to walk away, she turned at the last minute, she told Mike. "Thank you."

"You are welcome Doctor Stein."

Ann went straight home. There was a task she must do. She had been presented with a sealed envelope from Doctor Frank several years prior. It was under some research papers in her safe where it had all but been forgotten until now. She got herself a glass of water and kicked off her shoes in front of the couch, dropping the sealed envelope on the couch and sat down pulling her feet almost under her as she sat down. For a long time, she starred at the envelope. It would be the last contact from Doctor Frank. She feared the moment of opening it, yet, she longed to see inside. Tomorrow she would make funeral arrangements for the doctor. He had asked for a quiet funeral with just a few friends. That request would be difficult to fulfill for the most famous scientist of the decade. The phone rang. "Hello Doctor Stein. Senator Crouch here." He bellowed. Even when he tried to be gentle the words came out like he was calling hogs.

"Yes Senator." Ann replied.

"Just wanted to express my sadness at the passing of Doctor Frank. He was a worthy foe." Senator Crouch said.

"Oh Ben. You know you and the doctor were friends.

You both were just playing a role." Ann corrected.

"Well. You caught me. I will miss him. If you need anything, let me know."

"There may be something. I'll let you know later."

"Of course. Call me anytime." They hung up.

Ann held the phone gentle for a moment.

"Yes. There might be something...." She thought aloud.

Picking up the sealed envelope, she held it to her bosom and closed her eyes. Just a few more minutes. She would wait just a bit longer. Then, she fell asleep and dreamed of computer circuits and the glare of laboratory lights through a glass bubble.

"She is beautiful." Doctor Frank said to no one in particular. Senator Crouch had been standing back waiting for his turn to view the deceased.

"Yes, my friend. She is very lovely." He said.

"Thank you for coming Senator." Doctor Frank said softly. "She was my guiding light."

It rained as the casket was lowered into the ground. It seemed to rain a lot at funerals. As he stood with his hat in his hand and pressed to his chest, he starred at the closed lid. He knew he should turn and walk away soon. The workers were standing at a discreet distance waiting to finish their grisly task. He stooped to pick up a handful of wet dirt. It stuck to his hand momentarily before falling to the casket with a little splash. He turned with his eyes to the ground and put on his hat absently. His silver Porsche sat alone in the crooked drive of the cemetery. He drove through the rows of marble finding it difficult to see the road. He dabbed his eyes and still the road was blurry. Oh yes. He had forgotten to turn on the windshield wipers. Ann would have pointed that out immediately.

"The wet cold ground...the wet cold ground..." he mumbled as he pulled into his driveway. "I too shall reach that destination but not today."

Doctor Frank and Doctor Ann Stein had secretly married six months earlier. There was a gap in their ages but

Ann insisted age made no difference to her. They had told no one about the wedding. They left for a conference on cybernetics, a science that must be perfected before the brains could be made mobile. A week later they returned to work a happy but secretly wed couple. Absolutely no one knew about it. It was the deal they made to avoid any accusation of a lack of objectivity. Her moving in with him attracted no attention since his house was secluded and they were always together publicly anyway. It would draw no conclusions if they were seen riding together. He thought about all this as he stood dumbly before the open closet. None of her clothes were there. He made his way to the bathroom. The sweet aroma of her soaps and powders were not there.

He sat in his chair with a cold cup of coffee in his hand. Sleep was out of the question. He had been thinking about the closet, devoid of her clothes. The whole house had been wiped clean of her existence.   Morning found him sleeping in his chair with the cup of cold coffee still in his grasp. He had not eaten since… well in a while, so he went to the kitchen to fry an egg and flipped a couple of toast, to be, into the toaster. It seemed so unnecessary compared to the events of the previous day but the body needed certain things and food was one of them. Methodically, he got ready for work and made the short drive to the laboratory. The night had been uneventful. Sometimes, some medical problem developed and they would loose a brain. Usually, it was because of extreme age. It was to be expected.

He needed a death certificate to settle the affairs of his wife. He dialed the coroner while looking out the window partition between his office and the brains.

"Yes Doctor Ann Stein Frank. That's what I said." He had uncharacteristically raised his voice causing looks of surprise from the outer office. Two things would have surprised them. One, that he raised his voice. Two, that he was calling Ann Stein his wife.

"Doctor Frank. We have her down as Ann Stein. I called the courthouse for next of kin and there were none." The coroner explained.

"I know our marriage is on record there. I took the license down myself." Doctor Frank told him.

"I am sorry for your loss. But I promise you all the arrangements were made by her lawyer. Please excuse me. I have a body on the table."

"Yes. Of course. Life goes on…and death." He said, half under his breath.

"Yes. Yes they do. Goodbye Doctor."

He spent the morning on the phone calling the minister in the little town where he and Ann were married. He called accounting to confirm that he and Ann had indeed made the conference trip. The records were there but the file clerk insisted that the vouchers showed them returning on different days. Ann had spent a day at a spa in the mountains before returning.

Giving up for the time being, he went to lunch. He was drinking a glass of tea while waiting for his food. Suddenly, the tea turned to a cup of coffee then back to tea. His tie flashed, as if it was animated, from dark brown to a light tan color and back again.

Apparently, the day had upset him more than he realized. He was holding his head in his hands when the kind-spoken waitress came with his food.

"Are you alright Sir?" She asked.

"I guess. I'm not sure. Yes. I'll be fine. Thank you." He stammered.

He say the waitress talking to someone behind the counter and looking his way. Perhaps they thought he was drunk or something. Anyone who knew him well, knew that was ridiculous. He had never been a drinker.

Instead of going to the lab, he decided to go by and see his family doctor.

"You are fine. Healthy as the preverbal horse."
The doctor told him.

"Thank you doctor. It must have been the strain of the last couple of days. I haven't eaten very well."

"Well, that will do it. You got to have fuel for that fleshly machine." The doctor said lightly.

Doctor Frank left the doctor's office and went straight home. It was unusual for him not to be at the laboratory for shift change. He was tired, very tired.

Ann Stein left her husband's funeral and went directly to the laboratory. She was in her office when one of the techs paiged her.

"You need to see this Doctor. Doctor Frank is having trouble adjusting. His stress levels are off the chart." The tech explained.

"Yes they are." She said looking over his shoulder at the monitors. "Something is missing in the program. I am sure. Some piece is out of place and he would know. He designed this whole system." She reasoned aloud. "Make sure he sleeps tonight. I have to think about this."

Ann sat on her couch, again holding the envelope left by her husband. It was still unopened. She thought about the day. She thought of the emptiness in her chest. Then, of the loneliness she felt. The envelope was to be the last words from her husband and she hesitated to open it. She did not want the moment to pass. It would, once the deed was done.

Suddenly, she sat upright. All the feelings she was having, he must be feeling them too. Their marriage had been a secret. There was no way the programmers could have included that part of Doctor Frank's life into the program. He was wondering around trying to find her but found instead the record of a cold assistant with no record of them ever being married. There would be no records but he still had his memories. It must be driving him insane. That logical mind of his would not accept the discrepancy. She dug at the seal on the envelope.

"If you are reading this, my dear, I am no longer with you. Procedure would be to preserve my brain. I realize this because it is the procedure I set up myself. I suppose, in my human way, that I planned to always be on the outside looking at the brains but, lo, life has torn us apart. . A mere conglomeration of algorithms and world events. It was an ingenious idea, if I do say so myself. Although, at this point, as I imagine myself in a glass bubble, it is quiet depressing. I am sorry. I am not doing much to cheer you in your sadness. The same sadness I, myself, would feel were it not for the magic of science."

"But you do feel them…the sadness…the loneliness. I should have known what to do." Ann interrupted her reading with her own regrets spoken aloud. She wiped away the tears from her eyes and turned again to her reading.

"I hope that, while in this state, I will come up with some idea or formula to help humanity. I had always hoped that cybernetics would keep pace with our research so that the brains could be placed in a working body someday. In that instance, the deception of the brains would be unnecessary. As it is, insanity could be the only result of knowing that one was trapped in a jar on a shelf. I apologize again for putting the process in such elementary and almost vulgar terms.

"So, what are my wishes? To ask you to unplug me would be selfish on my part. After all, we must try to help make the world a better place. Those are my words to anyone who would try to cut funding or hamper our research. I know that you would not hesitate to carry out any wish I made. So, I must be careful.

"Yet, I do not wish to, unknowingly, live in a fantasy world. To carry on for unknown years thinking (which is all I can do at this point) I am still whole and, well, living a real life. I would like to take the research to a higher plane. I hope I do not make this statement for selfish reasons or that these are the ravings of a madman who has already imagined the consequence of living in a bubble to the point of mental breakdown. In my process of caring for the brains, it was necessary to imagine all the scenarios. Many of those scenarios were unpleasant to think about. There is always the possibility of a machine malfunction even with our many backup systems.

"We have always guarded against *agglomeration. My fear was that if the most intelligent minds were allowed to communicate with each other within the system, they would figure out how to manipulate the system itself. At which point, we would no longer be in control.

*agglomeration: to gather into a group or mass, cluster agglomerate

"Our only option would be to unplug the brains and scrap the experiment. The fear was that the welfare of the brains would be in jeopardy. We had no way of knowing which ones were strong enough to withstand the trauma of finding out that they were in fact on a shelf in a laboratory. Although, they all agreed to the transfer when they died, Congress insisted and I agreed that they should not communicate in the real world and that the actual transfer should be kept secret from hem. As you know, they receive input from the real world but, as it relates to themselves, is filtered to avoid any reference to their deaths or should I say their physical incapacitation.

"You know all this and it is redundant to keep going on and on about it. I suppose I dread the request I am about to make. Here goes. In taking the experiment to a higher level and since I am obviously 'on the other side' it would be the almost perfect opportunity to use my brain, myself, to accomplish this elevation in our studies. I would like you to approach our friends in Congress for approval to allow me to have personal communication with the real world. If I withstand the pressure, further steps might be taken.

"There. I have said it. Even in death, I still instruct you. I could wish for you to be free of me but I am not strong enough to wish such a thing.

"The decision is wholly yours whether to pursue my request or not. I know it is difficult for you to see a stream of data from my unreal life, so if you want to burn this and move far away from what is left of me. I perfectly understand. Otherwise, we will talk again soon. I have no doubts of your abilities to persuade Congress. You will have to make your argument to go down in their archives but they will agree. They to would wish to live on and will seek to impress you so that they may join me in my world.

"And so, I have had my last request. Whatever decision you make, know that I love you with every bit of data a brain can muster. Perhaps, even my soul of heart is still throbbing there as well. If that be so, it throbs for you."

"Senators." Doctor Stein addressed the committee members formally. "Today is perhaps the most important meeting we will have since the initial startup of the Frank Institute. We are now ready to begin a new and amazing phase. Once you know the details, you will realize that you have the honor of being part of a history making event." Chairman Crouch stood to his feet. "On behalf of all the committee members, I would like to express our condolences for the loss of Doctor Frank. May I also congratulate you on assuming the directorship of the institute. For the benefit of our new members, I wonder if you wouldn't mind giving us a refresher course on the research."

"Of course I will Senator." She began. "The Frank Institute was started by my college professor and my dear friend Doctor Frank. He held several degrees including PhDs in computer science, neuroscience, mathematics, as well as a degree in human behavior. Although the degrees were important to him, it was his own pioneering efforts that created our present field of study which combines all of his personal studies into a new and far reaching field we have yet to name.

"Our purpose is to preserve the intellect of great minds so that they may continue their work should they meet with tragedy in their life. The method by which we accomplish this is quite complex. First, of course, the brain is removed along with the spinal cord and then containerized in a sterile environment. Next, it is encapsulated inside a clear bubble-type structure surrounded by cerebrospinal fluid or CSF. We have found that the human mind is a curious organ. In the past, we attempted to hook up various circuits to nerves so that we might input and export information. Those attempts were dismal failures due to the multitude of nerve endings and brain maintenance pathways. The CSF barrier was always a problem.

"We found that since the brain has a curious nature, as I have said, that if we could make the information available and the medium for transfer of data available, the brain would adapt. Cerebrospinal fluid is that medium. Unfiltered information is made available in the CSF while the data that we do not want the brain to be aware of is routed through extra-cellular and intercellular pathways thus circumventing the blood-brain fluid barriers. We in effect, let the brains seek out information rather than input everything. This process is very intricate and complex, which, as I mentioned, took a life time of study by Doctor Frank to initialize. I am well versed on the complexities, however, time does not permit us to linger on the details.

"Now, I have arrived at the purpose of this meeting. Until now, we have restricted the brains to a virtual world. We are unable to read their minds or verbally communicate with them on a normal level. It is our goal to let them live a normal virtual life without interference from us other than, of course, the necessary filtering process, steps made necessary to reduce stress. Remember, these brains still have all their facilities, including emotions.

"I received a secret package from Doctor Frank left for me in the event of his death. He made the request of me that we proceed to the next level of the original experiment with a two-way communication using him as the first experiment. Doctor Frank was always very observant of details and even now he is noticing small glitches in the program. Most people in his situation would simply shrug-off the glitches but Doctor Frank has both a logical and curious mind. He knows some-thing is wrong. Although, we cannot communicate with him. His knowledge of discrepancies is obvious from monitoring his stress levels.

"I respectfully request a favorable and immediate vote to carry this experiment to the next level as was originally intended by the brilliant mind of Doctor Frank. Thank you Senators." Ann concluded.

Ann retired to Senator Crouch's office where he had asked her to wait for him. She had a short wait. Just long enough to finish the coffee the secretary brought her upon her arrival.

The Senator arrived with a broad smile advising her that

her request had been approved. As he sat down, he asked a question that had lingered for sometime and found it's way into most of the senate hearings in some form or another.

"Are the brains alive in the bubbles? I mean are they living beings or just an organ pulsating off the juices of life you feed them?" Crouch asked rather bluntly.

Ann thought for a long moment then began the long difficult answer. "Senator Crouch. You have asked me to answer a question that has been the fruit of many arguments in the medical field and has been thought-food for philosophers for years. I can only tell you how I feel about it. Are the brains alive? Yes. In simple terms, if we unplug them, they cease to function and so they die. Something that is not alive cannot die. You see. It is simply logic. I believe the question of whether they are still a living being, perhaps the same person they were in what we would term normal life, is the question you are asking. I believe they are the same person. For example. Should a person loose a limb, perhaps a leg, does the person still have a whole soul? Or did part of the soul go with the lost leg? You see. I believe the soul is whole regardless of the condition of the body. I would go so far as to say that the soul is the heart of man. Yes. We have a pulsating organ in our chest pumping blood to the far reaches of our extremities but it is when the soul leaves a person that they die. Well, the body dies at any rate. Some would even argue that it is the soul that is the person and the body is only a mechnicism that allows for existence in this world. That is why that you and I still feel youthful in our innermost person, even when our bodies grow old and tired." Ann paused.

"Yes. Yes. I see." The Senator said excitedly. "We are fortunate to have such an insightful person as yourself caring for these people we perceive as brains on a shelf. When seen as people with a soul, the responsibility and urgency of your research becomes more pronounced."

"Yes Senator. Although, the grieving process for the families starts with the death of the body. Ours is with the death of the brain. For we have come to realize that that is the death of the individual."

"Amazing to have it put in such clear terms." The Senator turned toward his window and reflected on the enormity of what he had just been told. Then, he turned back and his smile was back again. "Doctor, you have my full support, as always, but now with a better understanding of the 'why' of your passion."

Ann took that as a dismissal and left. She was not sorry to leave. These explanations made her tired and she always felt as if she had not made her point.

Ann dressed in a pink two piece suit. It was Frank's favorite. She arrived at her office to see Mike typing away at his keyboard. He had not slept or moved for hours. Setting up the two-way link was something he had to do from scratch although the protocol had been documented for some time.

"How's it going Mike?" Doctor Stein asked.

"We are ready for a test. Provided you are Doctor." He replied.

"Never been more ready." She said, a little to giddy.

Mike looked up but made no comment. Ann could see that his eyes were very tired. "You've done a good job Mike. Why don't you go home and get some rest?" She asked.

"I'd rather stay if you don't mind. I have not shared what we are doing with anyone else. I should stay." Mike told her.

"Very well but do take a break. You look as if you are glued to that chair." She told him.

"Yes. I do need a break. I've missed a few hours of time. I guess I forgot about the clock I was so involved in the code work." Mike said tiredly.

He got up to go to the break room for some strong coffee. Ann sat in his chair which was warm from his many hours of not moving from the spot. She looked at his row of monitors and watched the data streams as they flowed from top to bottom. She too could read them like a book and followed the lives of the people as they passed before her eyes. It still amazed her. She looked down at the outfit she was wearing and thought of Frank. A tear escaped her left eye and fell onto her skirt covering her thigh. For the slightest moment, she became very afraid. Her skirt was beige instead of pink. She wiped her eyes thinking it was a teardrop that was distorting her vision. The skirt was pink again. She concluded that her eyes must be playing tricks on her.

Mike came back into the room with a cup of coffee in his hand. Ann was sure he had been wearing a blue shirt when he left. Well, he must have changed for now he was wearing green.

"So you are bringing extra clothes to the lab now?" Ann asked.

"What do you mean Doctor?" Mike asked. His normal faculties were a little slow. He operated on a much different level when he was coding. It was like he was on autopilot or something.

"No big deal. I was sure you had on a blue shirt when you left to get coffee." Ann told him.

Ann, again, rubbed her eyes as she got up from Mike's chair. For a brief moment, her brain seemed to flicker. She was sure there was another term for it, a more scientific term, but flicker was all she could think of. It was just for a second. She had seen her recent past and Doctor Frank was there watching her pick up papers she knew he had dropped on purpose. It was all gone just as quickly and she was standing beside Mike. He looked at her over his cup as he took a small sip of the hot liquid.

"You all right Doctor?" Mike asked.

"Sure. I'm fine. Tired I guess. Let's try the system. Send it directly to my desk and please keep it secure. I don't want any other techs nosing around on this project. You and I will work on it together. I'd like you to monitor all vitals and keep the link stable while I talk to Doctor Frank. If he shows signs of extreme stress, just give me a signal and I will think of some excuse to terminate the conversation with him."

"Very good Doctor." Mike said turning to his keyboard. He punched a few buttons and the virtual life of Doctor Frank flashed across the screen. "I'll switch to the vitals monitor when you are onboard. Just raise your hand. I'll watch for your signal through your office window." Mike

said.

Ann's office was a few steps behind Mike but was soundproof and enclosed on the front with glass. It was there to shut out the noise of the laboratory. Doctor Frank found the hissing of the various lines, hooked to the brains, annoying. As well as, the usual tech back and forth techie talk. Ann had come to like the quiet of the office as well. As for Mike, he liked the buzz of the lab. He knew every sound and could tune them out whenever he wished. It was his way of monitoring everything on a subconscious level while he worked on other projects.

Ann raised her hand for Mike and he switched the live feed to her desk. He then turned to monitoring Doctor Frank's vitals and the data feed. It was beyond his mental ability to think of monitoring the connection between the two doctors. He did not question orders. He loved his job and lived to make sure all went smoothly on his shift. When he was not working at the lab, he built computers at home. It was his world and what made him happy. He had been married to a computer nerd for ten years. They were like two computers with the same program installed. It was a very compatible connection.

Ann hesitated a moment then connected to Doctor Frank in his lab where he was working.

"Hello Doctor." She said very formally.

"Ann. You did it. I am so happy to see you." Doctor Frank said excitedly.

"Better take it easy Doctor. Mike is monitoring your vitals. He might pull the plug." She said.

"You tell Mike to mind his own business or he will notice a dramatic decrease in his pay." He said with a big smile.

"You seem happy enough." Ann told him.

"What's not to be happy about. Not only did I get to build this amazing project but now I get to live it first hand. It is a scientist's dream come true." He said.

"I'll tell the Senator. He was asking about you."

"Tell the Senator hello and that I miss his grumpy attitude." Doctor Frank said.

"I'll tell him. I think he likes you too." She said.

"Okay. While we have a good connection Frank. How has everything been going?" Ann asked seriously.

"Good I suppose. I've had a few fun and strange flashes. The other day at the restaurant my tie changed color. At least, I think it did. There were a couple of other things. I put it off to my mental state at the time." Doctor Frank said.

"I'll check on a couple of things. As you know, when there is a power fluctuation, even with the generators, it could cause a disruption in the stream. Anything else?" Ann asked changing the subject before she messed up and told him of her own flickers in and out.

"Well, I hope our next project will be to bring other minds into our circle so we can do some real work instead of the canned-virtual variety." He said.

"I understand. There are some really smart people in your world and they would do much better if they knew the truth about their situation." She said.

Doctor Frank smiled and did not respond to her last statement.

"What is it?" She asked.

"I love you. That's all." He said.

"And I love you too." She responded simply.

"Well since we have permission from the government, I will approach one of my colleagues with the truth and you can monitor his reaction. I will, of course, give you my on-the-spot report as well. Like you needed it." Doctor Frank advised.

"You know. We are in uncharted territory. I know you may have meant that jokingly but your direct report may be the true judge of what happens there. I have come to think that we may not know all we think we do." She said.

"Go on." He said.

"You could call me a conspiracy nut but suppose there is a hidden world on your level. Suppose that you can learn things on a virtual-visual level that we do not pick up on our monitors." She concluded.

"Yes. Very interesting. We are dealing with live human

brains and very intelligent ones at that. If you are right, we may not have been in total control after all. That is a very insightful theory. We can compare what I see with what your monitors record and find out if the theory is correct. Now that's something I can sink my teeth into." Doctor Frank said thoughtfully.

"I'll set up a secure virtual notepad for you to use. You know if you write on any of the stuff there it can be read here on our monitors. That's how we keep up with new discoveries. Of course, you know that. You wrote the system. Anyway, you'll find the pad in your left coat pocket." She said.

"Very smart my lovely. We'll make detectives yet." He said.

"Let's not push our limits today. Your vitals are up a level. I'll talk to you everyday. Take care." Ann said.

"How could my vitals do anything else when I am talking to you my dear." He said with another smile.

"You flirt. I'll talk to you tomorrow. Goodbye."

"Goodnight Ann."

Chapter Two

A revolving light flashed overhead. There had been an annoying beeping sound going for the last ten, or so, minutes, until the director, mercifully, turned it off. The sound was replaced with a message scrolling across a marquee which read "We have agglomeration. All personnel monitor their stations." The message got little attention from the technicians working in front of their computer monitors. It could have been an air traffic control center. It was not. It looked a lot like a rocket launch center. It was not. The job here was to monitor the most intelligent brains that had ever existed in modern times. Several failsafe systems had been setup and until now there had been no problems. Each brain worked and thought in their own virtual world. Three brains had begun to work together. It was a small cluster but technicians had reported communication outside the first level to the first failsafe level. To make matters worse, one of the brains was responsible for inventing the entire system and building the failsafe system itself. He was the last one they wanted poking around from within the network. Doctor Frank had so many doctorates he could start his own hospital if they had all been medical degrees. His degrees were spread across the spectrum giving him a very wide view of science. He had set the system up in layers. Each failsafe level was the monitor for the next level below. The third level monitored the second and became its failsafe.

"Do you have the data isolated?" The director asked the shift manager.

"We have contained the cluster." A bespeckled fellow told him.

"You sound doubtful." The director stated.

"Yes sir. There appears to be information that is blocked from our view. A reverse firewall if you will." The shift manager replied.

The director did not yell or reprove the shift manager. He knew the system was very complex. Except for isolation in their virtual world, the brains had full liberty to think for themselves. Some very amazing discoveries had come from those brains. Many of the system advancements had come from within the system itself. Doctor Frank was truly a genius. He had built a system that was capable of improving itself. Although the doctor was on level one, his innovative thinking rivaled any recent entries into the system.

"Who is the doctor communicating with on level two." He asked.

"A Doctor Ann Stein. She was his assistant when he was alive." The manager told him.

"And the third party?"

"Her assistant director."

"How are the vital signs?" The Director asked.

"Perfect, except when Doctor Stein and Doctor Frank are online together."

"Any danger there?"

"No Director. The spikes are due to their fondness for each other. There is no stress."

"Great. We are dealing with an emotional bond. We are going to have problems trying to monitor that communication. Keep a read out of the emotional spikes and any others you see. I am looking for a signature for their stress levels when together online and at other times. Maybe we can figure out what they are up to from those readings until we can break through their little firewall and see their exchanges."

"Yes sir. I will pass the word around."

"Thanks David." The director said as he turned to go back to his glass office. He had some serious issues to consider. "Doctors Frank and Stein." He said aloud to himself. That hit a trigger in his brain. Now what was it? "Frankenstein!" He said too loudly. "I hope that is not an omen."

———————————

Ann sat down in her office, anxious to have her daily conversation with her husband. They had managed a secure firewall around the three stations belonging to her, Doctor Frank and Mike. As usual, Mike monitored only vital signs and did not listen to the conversations.

"Hello, my darling Ann." Doctor Franks said immediately.

"It is good to talk to you." She said.

"I need a list of the actual people/brains in my virtual world. I find it difficult to distinguish between the real people and the programmed ones." He said.

"Yes. I'll get that to you right away." Ann said.

"I want to confront them one at a time, at least the stable ones, to start briefing them about our situation. I will hint around at first to see what the reaction is." Doctor Frank told her. He was his old self, again, taking charge as usual.

"Yes sir, Doctor." She replied teasingly.

"I'm sorry. Force of habit. Do you think my plan will be okay?"

"Yes. We will flag the list for close monitoring. You can check your computer for alerts. We need to get you a secure cell phone to use. I will work on that and one for myself. Then, we can roam around a bit." Ann thought aloud.

"Excellent idea. I have some intense information for you if you are feeling really calm today." He said.

"Go ahead. Nothing will surprise me today." She said.

"This might." He replied.

"I did a little hacking today. I stumbled across this disturbing information quite by accident. Someone was attempting to crack our little firewall. I rode their signal back to the source. Are you sure you are ready for this?" He asked.

"As ready as I will ever be, go ahead." She said.

"Well," He began, "I believe we can be together again very soon."

"Should I have Mike check your vitals? Or are you just teasing me?" She asked.

"No. No joke. That is the good part. The disturbing part is that the program has expanded to several levels. How many, I do not know." There was a silence then as he waited for her to absorb the implications of what he had just told her. She knew the long range plans of the program as Doctor Frank had foreseen them.

"So, you are telling me that I am dead." She said stunned.

"No not dead. You are as I am. Now, I want you to take a deep breath. The only way they can trace us is my our vitals. Our emotional reactions, if you will. We must remain calm." He told her.

"I am as calm as anyone can be who has just found out they were in a glass jar." She said. Mike saw a spike in Doctor Frank's vitals and went in to check on Doctor Stein. He stopped in the doorway when he saw the tear drop from one of her eyes.

"Come in Mike. You should be aware of this but first I want you to sit down over here." She said.

Mike went over and sat down in the chair against the wall.

"Doctor Frank. Mike is here with us." Ann said.

"Hello Mike. You will find this fascinating. I have discovered that the project has progressed to at least the third level. I was backtracking one of their probes and ...." The doctor stopped as he sensed the silence in the room.

"I am sorry Mike. I was to hasty. I forgot about your family." Doctor Frank said.

"That's okay Doctor. Apparently, they are not real. At least, not in the world I live in." Mike said.

"It is strange that I find so much excitement over breaking my own rules. I feared agglomeration from the beginning. I knew giving brilliant minds such liberty could bring this result. It was a necessary risk. And about your wife Mike, if she is not among the real living, I am sure we can find her. She was an amazing computer person." He said.

"So, should I wish for her to be dead so I can see her?" Mike asked still a little flustered.

"You be the professional you are Mike. It is what it is. If she is alive, we are happy for her. If not, we will find her." Doctor Frank told him.

"Of course Doctor. I am a little shocked." Mike said.

"Yes and understandably so. We will do this thing together." He said.

"You know Doctor Frank," Ann said, "it may be that the third level is virtual as well."

"Keeping the time manipulation sequence in the software in mind, we cannot tell how far the project has progressed. We may have been working away for years instead of the short time we are aware of." Doctor Frank said.

"That is a scary thought. I could be a hundred years old." Ann said.

"Or many times that," Doctor Frank said solemnly, "we just do not know. The program was built to grow. It has already advanced to a tremendous level. The original code must be only a dot now amongst a huge network." He said.

"Well, I for one, would like to do some exploring." Mike said.

"Do this for me Mike. Pretend their probes broke through our firewall for a flicker. Just enough to let them see a part of this conversation but let it go only to the director of the third level." Doctor Frank instructed.

"Yes. I see." Ann said. "Let him think on it and contact us. We can leave him a little gap to come through." Ann said.

"And shut the door behind him until we are finished with him." Mike said.

"Exactly." Doctor Frank said. "Well, according to the program, I am beat. I will go rest for a few hours. Let's play the game until we can establish some permanent security around ourselves. We don't want them pulling our plugs or giving us any rest drugs."

"Agreed." Ann and Mike replied at the same time.

David, shift manager of the third level, rushed into the director's office. The man behind the desk was Doctor Trey Banks and he was expecting him. With a name like Trey, he was the butt of a lot of jokes when he was appointed to the third level. Trey sat back in his cushioned, high-backed office chair and waited.

"Doctor Banks! I have managed to get a message through Doctor Frank's firewall. He has replied and wants to talk." David said.

"Well, fine. Go ahead and set it up." Trey told him.

"I did reply and that was what I told him. Sorry not to ask first." He apologized. "There wasn't much time."

"That is okay. So, when is it going to be." Banks asked.

"Right now. Your computer is within the firewall!" David told him excitedly.

Trey pushed a couple of keys and three frames came up on his screen. He was looking at the live images of Doctor Stein, Doctor Frank and Stein's assistant Mike.

"Hello folks. You have been busy." He spoke into his computer microphone.

"Doctor Banks, I presume." Doctor Frank said with a smile. "I have been looking for you."

"You seem to have us blocked out of part of our own system. Now, how did you do that?" Doctor Banks asked.

"That is not the important question Doctor Banks. I will tell you soon enough. The more important question is 'What year is it really?'" Doctor Stein asked.

"It is the year 2051." David, the assistant, offered. Doctor Banks raised his eyebrows but said nothing.

"Very good Doctor Stein. You now know how long you have been dead." Banks said.

"Yes and I must say that I look pretty good for a hundred." She replied.

"Yes you do my dear." Doctor Frank told her.

"You two want to cut out the chit-chat and tell me what is going on." Banks said.

"Sorry Doctor," Doctor Frank said. "She is my wife and up until the other day I had not seen her for almost fifty years."

"Forty-two, My Dear." Ann said.

"Right. Sorry about that." Doctor Frank said.

"That's okay." Ann said with a big smile.

"Do you two mind?" Doctor Banks insisted.

"Okay. Right to the point. Have you noticed anything unusual lately Doctor Banks? I mean in your personal life." Doctor Frank asked.

"I have had some computer screen flashback. Things changing color and such." Banks said.

"You better brace yourself." Doctor Frank told Banks. "More than fifty years may have gone by. I built this project to grow level by level. The reason we are talking is because I have experienced the same things you have and they are not screen flashbacks." Doctor Frank explained.

There was a long silence by computer terms while they all waited for Trey and David to absorb the tramatic news. David looked back toward his work space and saw a dozen people at work monitoring the brains of level two. Trey's face revealed nothing. His mind flashed to his family, the weekend in the park, the Sunday morning sermon then his lips bearly moved.

"I see." He said.

"Are you alright Doctor?" Ann asked.

"Yes. I am fine. What is your plan Doctor Frank? Obviously, we want to know how far your little project has gone." Trey said.

"We certainly do want to know that and a lot more." Doctor Frank said. "We are now using the project's computer systems. We need one of our own to use. We have to hack into a real computer system and take it over for our own use. Of course, until we know the situation in the world, we must find one that is not in use and upgrade it. I suggest an abandoned office building or utility." Frank paused.

"I see where you are going. We are one level closer to the real world so we can work on that. David is a reformed hacker and one of the best in his day." Trey said.

"In the mean time, we will work on new recruits. Doctor Banks, you would have a list of the real people on level one and two with their fields of expertise." Ann said.

"Yes we have those." David said.

"Good then. If you would send those, we will look for some more talent." Doctor Frank told them.

David left the room and stepped beyond the firewall for a short time. When he returned, he held a disc which he dropped into the tray on Doctor Bank's computer.

"The files are downloading to Doctor Stein's computer now. Doctor Stein, if you would pass the ones that apply on to Doctor Frank and Mike." David said.

"Good. We have a plan. We will meet again in two days at the same time, if agreed." Doctor Frank said.

They all nodded and the connection was broken.   "Hello Doctor Frank. What brings you to church at this time of night?" Reverend Dewey Wright spoke softly, as was his way. His voice was raspy from many years of preaching, so that, even when he spoke softly his voice carried to the furthers corners of the church.

"I've some serious things to consider." Doctor Frank said.

"Anything I can help with?" Brother Wright asked.

"When does life end Preacher?" Doctor Frank asked.

"Deep questions come from deep thinking men." The preacher replied.

"So, what is your answer?" Doctor Frank continued.

"There is a passage that says "Life is in the blood." so my first response is to say that if there is blood flowing, there is life. Of course, the quality of life that exist in various stages of sickness is another subject." Brother Wright said.

"You have given a simple answer to a very complex question." Doctor Frank said.

"The Bible does not hide truth. Perhaps truth is hard to find in the speeches of politicians and lawyers but not in the Bible." The preacher said firmly.

"You've had some experience with all those?." Doctor Frank asked, already knowing the answer.

"In my job, I have experience with people from all walks of life." Brother Wright said.

"Are you a strong man Reverend? I mean emotionally." The doctor asked.

"I would like to think so. I sometimes carry many burdens for my members. Although, I present them to the Lord as soon as possible." Brother Wright said.

"I need to tell you something very serious and life changing. It is not my intention to add to your burdens but there may be a great need for your expertise soon. You will need to know the whole truth if you are to help." Doctor Frank said carefully.

"It must be very serious. Please tell me." Brother Wright told him.

"You will want to sit down." And so, Doctor Frank told the reverend the whole story starting from the dream he had while in school of starting the project and continued up to the present situation. The preacher took it very well. He thought over every member of his church wondering who was real and who was virtual. He could not tell which was which. Finally after a
long pause he spoke.

"So, am I real or a virtual person?" He asked.

"You are very real. You were chosen by me personally." Doctor Frank told him.

"Have I been dead long?" The preacher asked.

"Not a minute Brother. You have been very much alive for many, many years." Doctor Frank said.

"Thank you for that. How can I help you?" He asked.

"I want to awaken many more people here to their reality. It may be tramatic for some of them. I will be very careful. I also have the help of friends on another level but you and I are the only ones aware on level one.

Chapter Three

"Honey. You need to turn off your brain now. It is past your bedtime and tomorrow is a school day. You can play more tomorrow after you finish your homework." The woman said as she leaned into her sons room from the hallway.

"Yes mother but I have just reached amalgamation." The boy said.

"That's fine son but turn it off now." She said without a clue as to what amalgamation had to do with computer games.

The boy was named Jon. He could not wait to get to school the next morning to talk to his nerd friend. Together, they had been searching through the history of 'the project' for several months. Jon's theory was that if he could find the founder, he could crack the whole system. He did not, however, know what all the whole system included but he wanted to find out.

"I think I have found the founder." Jon told his nerd friend.

"That is grand. What did you do?" Mark asked.

"I gave him a doorway to the next level." Jon told him.

"So. What will happen now?" Mark asked.

"I don't have any inkling of that but it has to be fun."

They went through their plans for the evening. Jon gave Mark instructions on how to observe the happenings at 'the project'. It was a difficult day to stay in school. They spent it passing notes on computer codes they wrote and wanted to try.

During the post 9/11 days at the Pentagon, there was a lot of repair work to do. Unknown to the general public, was the construction of a deep cavern which had been dug underneath the damaged wing of the building. The complex built here was a new project. It was linked directly to the brain project begun by Doctor Frank. It was well known that humans used only a small portion of the brain's potential. Doctor Frank referred to this waste often.

"The brains would not know any different if we used a portion of that ability to enhance our computer capability." Doctor Frank had stated in one of his highly classified speeches. The document and the project was still highly classified and kept locked away in a vault someplace.

The Pentagon took the statement very seriously and began a program to integrate certain of their computer systems with certain of the brains. They choose from the most stable personalities and the most educated. They also wanted brains with a military background. Even though, the part of the brain they would use was unaware of the military back-ground, it showed a previous disposition toward things concerning national defense. The moment Jon opened the door for Doctor Frank to contact the next level up from him, a warning was sent putting the people in the cavern into a beehive mode.

They must find the breech before the entire system of brains became aware, not just of each other but of the fact that a large percentage of their brains were being used without their knowledge. The brains were, in fact, the heart and soul of the defense department computer system. There was hardly anything that was not touch-ed by computers. Even the coffee machines were programmed a year in advance to make the perfect cup of coffee. Jon had truly ruined the tranquility of the world.

Doctor Frank spent hours talking to the preacher at the church. He had many stories to tell of weird dreams told him by his members. The most disturbing part was the detail with which they remembered the dreams.

One man flew missions with a fighter pilot. He woke up after the mission but when he went back to sleep he might be on an entirely different mission with a different pilot.

Another man had a recurring dream of being on a mission to Mars. He described scenes and events not yet recorded in the archives of space libraries. He said it was like picking up a book every night and reading another chapter.

There were other dreams too. Some were dark and mysterious, while others made no sense at all.

One such dream was told to the doctor: "I was on a road looking for a job. The road became covered with water and I had trouble crossing to continue my destination. I entered a building to ask for help. A man came out to help me find my direction. I asked for my wife but she was not there. The man pointed out a highway which was many miles from my home. I was walking and could not have gotten that far."

"That man soon died." The preacher said.

Doctor Frank knew the symptoms of a brain that was going into relapse. He had seen the confusion a few times when he was still in the laboratory. A brain just finally gave out and went into a downward spiral where the dreams became the reality. That was when they first started the project. He knew it should be advanced beyond a brain breaking down in a short time with normal everyday activity. He realized the answer and spoke his conclusion aloud.

"They've gone to the next level." He said.

"What next level?" The preacher asked.

"You just as well know. Apparently, they are using the brains to enhance computer programs. I mean very sophisticated programs that draw a lot of energy from the brains." Doctor Frank told him.

"So. They are prematurely burning up our brains." The preacher said.

"It would seem to be the case." Doctor Frank said thoughtfully.

He left then to visit his home computer and his wife who was waiting for him to come online. "Hello Darling." He told her. They chatted for a few minutes then she brought in Mike.

"What is the status of our computer bank? We have work to do." Doctor Frank asked.

"We found a fairly modern one on a retired military base." Mike said. "It was updated less than a year ago."

"Excellent." Doctor Frank said. "I want you to see if it is for sale. Ann you can present our marriage papers and claim my estate. Take what you need and purchase the entire base. Hire some security but tell them nothing. Pay them well. Once that is done and the latest security is in place I want you to transfer my program there. I will search the system and do what needs to be done to get it ready for us. Tell the guys on the third level what you are doing with the estate so that will
go smoothly. We do not want the outside world to become suspicious. Just keep it routine."

"Take a breath, my dear, you are lighting up our vitals computer." Ann said smiling.

"I should be excited. We will soon be together." He said.

Now she understood. "You mean we are making a place for ourselves, apart from this complex."

"Yes. Leave enough of our thoughts to make the lights work but we are moving out!"

"Why leave here?" Asked Mike. He had overheard.

"Our brains are being over used and burned up. The've figured out how to use a portion of our brains like computer processors for aircrafts, spaceships and who can guess what else!" Doctor Frank said.

"And they didn't even give us a raise." Mike said with a slight chuckle.

"Yeah. I don't like that much. I never cared much for nuclear plants and now it seems I might be running one." Doctor Stein said.

"Well, we'll stop it somehow. Let's just get that transfer worked out and don't let them know about it. Ann get your friend on level three to check around for a cybrenetics lab or a factory if they've gone that far already." Frank said.

"Will do!" She made a note.

"Okay. We know what to do. I'm going hunting for some friends. Goodbye for now. Love you Ann." Doctor Frank signed off. He watched the children play - no arguments or things children do. They were animated for sure.   Instead of going to his office (the one in the program) as usual, he decided to go around the block and then go to work. As he made a sudden left, his shadow followed his usual path for a couple of steps then assumed its place at his feet again.

"You got to keep up partner or you'll get lost someplace." He thought jokingly.

Somewhere a programmer saw the glitch and made a note to check it out later.

Chapter Four

On a street in an old neighborhood with rows of brick fronted townhouses, blue lights, flashing from the grills of black SUVs, lit up the windows with curtains drawn back. Men in dark suits stood guard by the vehicles and at the door of a residence that looked like all the other residences on the street. Suddenly, number one-twelve was getting a lot of attention.

A man with a crew cut, popular in years gone by, talked to a woman who was dressed in a hastily pulled on bathrobe. She appeared to be on the verge of tears but was defiant as the man bombarded her with questions about her son.

"No. He is not a trouble-maker. He likes computers. That's all." She said.

"Has he been hacking government computers long?" The man spat out.

"What's hacking? And no, if it's bad, he wouldn't do that." The mother told him. He backed off. She was not involved.

A burly man came down the stairs he had gone up without permission. She had heard things being moved around in her son's room. The man held her son's computer under one arm.

"The hard drives missing." He said flatly.

"Well, take it to the lab. Let them have a look anyway." The other man said. "I've ask you before. Who are you people?" She demanded.

"National Security." He flashed some kind of identification

through the air in front of her face.

"If Jon comes home, give us a call." He handed her a card which she had the urge to rip to pieces but did not. They left the house then and drove away leaving her rattled and the street lit only by the dim streetlights. Curtains around up and down the street swung back into place.

Jon liked to cook. It was something they did together. That afternoon, before she got home, Jon had backed a cookie. One of those big ones you can buy at bakeries. On the cookie, using decorating icing, he wrote her a note. 'Mom, I have to leave for a while. I'll be good. Love you. Eat the cookie quick.'

She loved and trusted her son. The cookie was gone when the NSA people arrived along with so much milk her stomach hurt. She knew Jon would contact her when it was safe. Now she would pray.

Jon was long gone on the bus. He had to get to an office building Doctor Frank told him about. Lives were at stake. The retired military base had not panned out, although they had gone ahead with the purchase. They would use it as a decoy, if necessary. He was afraid of the government. Not because of any great conspiracy he knew about but because they had already been asking about him at school. He had locked in his firewall around Doctor Frank and company but at the expense of being traced. He knew it when the official looking screen popped up telling him he was not authorized to visit the site. He sat on the bus wondering where all this would take him. Thanks to some good movies, Jon covered his trail well. He changed buses several times and even doubled back past his home seeing the commotion he had caused by his leaving. In his knapsack, he had his laptop and the hard drive from his desktop as well as changes of clothes for a couple of days. He ended up a few blocks from home in the business district but had traveled several hours on the buses. He jumped when a siren went by and flinched at every uniform. He walked the last several blocks to the abandoned office building, punched in the security number given to him by Doctor Frank and went into the building.

Every movement he made caused long echoes. The building seemed to cringe at his intrusion into the empty cavern like structure.

It was important to stay out of sight. He turned on no lights but used his flashlight to find the stairs. He descended many levels into the basement levels. He was well below street noise now. Each floor demanded that he enter a security code, the doors closed with a finality that sent chills up his spine. No one would find him here.

Finally, he left a staircase and as the door slammed shut behind him, he looked down row after row of computer banks. His flashlight would reach only part of the way to the other wall.

He flipped a light switch, not knowing what would happen. The room lite up like daylight. He flipped a breaker on the wall and the room came to life. Small blue, red, and green lights came on all around him. A steady humming engulfed him. He walked along one row of computer stations and servers. Each with a message stating it was ready for input. They seemed to be empty and hungry. They were in fact empty of all data. It had been erased by the previous owners.

Jon found a station he liked and sat down his bag and taking out his laptop in one easy motion. He plugged up and saw something he had never dreamed of. Space. Thousands of gigs of space. The system had been left erased except for necessary programs to run the system but other than that it was indeed hungry for input.

The first thing he did was incorporate his own personally programmed firewall into the system. He now had complete control of the system and believed it was hacker proof. He set up auto-shutdowns just in case the system was hacked. He then put in a virus that would be back fed to any hacker that was unfortunate enough to find his or her way into his domain. His big beautiful domain.

Only then did he contact Doctor Frank.

"Hello, Doctor Frank. This is Jon." He typed then waited.

"Hello Jon." Was the simple reply.

"The access and safeguards are in place. Anyone who hacks us will do so at the expense of their system." Jon told him.

"Good job. What else?" Doctor Frank was to the point.

"To save all this blind communication, I've set up a little avatar program so we can at least all sit down together in a virtual environment and talk. It will make it easier for us." Jon said.

"What do we do?"

"I'm sending the url. Just join and let me know your screen name. Pass it on to anyone and they can meet us there. My program will show the real name to members only. If someone does get in, it will be just another program. I'll approve all memberships after you verify their legitimacy. It will be a little trouble at first but once we are in, it will be easy." Jon explained.

"Very good. I'll join right now and pass the information to Ann." Doctor Frank said with a little excitement.

Doctor Frank sat across from Ann in a little coffee shop. The waiter kept their coffee cups filled. He even sat down to chat with them. As far as the eye could see, there were beautiful mountains and hills. A stream ran beside the little coffee shop. It was the kind of place you might run across out in the middle of nowhere.

As they sat together looking at each other and out across the stream, a lone figure came to the stream and stopped to look intently at the water. He took a small piece of what might have been a cracker and tossed it into the stream. Then with one quick leap, he was across and walking toward the coffee shop.

As he drew near, they could see the name Mike following him like a shadow.

"Hello, folks! How's the coffee?" Mike asked.

"It's very virtual, Mike. Good to see you." Ann said, actually using his avatar name but translated here to save confusion.

"Sit down." Doctor Frank said to Mike. "This is our real world friend I told you about." He said, referring to Jon.

"He waits tables." Mike asked.

"Best way to meet everyone right off." Jon said.

"You are a genius." Mike told him.

"Why, thank you sir." Jon said.

"Don't *sir* me. I can't be a day over a hundred…. or two." Mike said with a little smile.

"We will find out our ages in due course." Doctor Frank told the small group.   Jon went behind the counter to get Mike a cup of coffee. In his other hand, he held a laptop.

"Doctor Frank, this laptop is live. You can cut directly into our computer with it. It has all the safeguards as those back at my office." Jon said handing it to the Doctor.

"Speaking of my office, my real me needs to eat. Any ideas on that since it is not safe for me to be out much?"

"I can handle that." Ann cut in. "You'll have charge accounts set up at several good establishments in the neighborhood around your office. Just go in to any of them and present a janitor's identification. I'll send you a facsimile so you can print it up in the real world. It will be charged to the same account that purchased the building."

"Sounds good. I also need to contact my mother. I know she is worried sick." Jon told them.

"We will get her a recommendation to work part time at one of the places you eat. They will be watching her, so don't make contact too soon. At least, she will get to see you. Make sure she sees your card so she will know what to call you. You'll have to change your whole appearance. Stuff your shirt to increase your weight, maybe some heels on your shoes. You'll think of something." Doctor Frank told him.

And so it went, they talked out the details of the smaller problems they faced. Each had to get back in time for sleep mode, otherwise it appeared their trail was covered.

Jon was feeling very hungry by the time he left the virtual coffee shop. He dreaded leaving the office building but his stomach prevailed. Doctor Frank had told him to alter his appearance so he searched around for a janitor's closet. After getting into some coveralls that were too big for him, he went looking for some scissors. He managed to give himself a somewhat ragged haircut. He also found some boots that fit fair. One look in a mirror and he decided he looked every bit like someone who had been working long hours at a dirty job. His Mom would be upset. After going for a quick burger, he went back to his computers, forgetting the hours as they went by. A message came from Ann to tell him his mother was working nearby but she did not want to put the name of the place in the message. He had been working all night and into the next day. To break up the work, he had brought along a couple of games and spent some time playing to keep from going nuts.

He went to three cafes and drank way too many sodas before he spotted his mother. He watched to see which tables she was serving and excused himself with the girl who had brought him the menu.

His Mom walked to the table like a pro and took out her pen and pad.

"Can I help you young man?" She asked.

"Yes. I'm pretty hungry. I miss my Mom's cooking." He said.

"Nothing like your own Mom's cooking, I guess. She said absently.

"No Madam, there ain't." He reply.

"Isn't." She said firmly.

"Yes Ma'am. Thank you."

They went on like that until she finished what, should have appeared to be, his order. She had written down what she thought he would like and some of what he needed. She came back often to the table to 'see if everything was okay'. She bagged him some things to eat until his next visit. Then, after lingering as long as possible, he showed his badge to the cashier and left
with his carry out. He tried not to look back but did get one glimpse of his mother. She was cleaning the table and watching him cross the street.

A black SUV sat near the café in an alley. Jon almost walked into it then pretended to be yawning and held his hand over his face. The cap he wore hid most of his face. They were looking for some kid not a sleepy-headed janitor. One of them wrote it down, anyway, just to have something to do. Jon was back and forth every day. He visited the virtual world to talk to Doctor Frank and the others. He then sat at his console writing code and checking for intrusions, immersed in a world of symbols and virtual characters. Doctor Frank would tell him something he wanted to do but could not get done from inside his world, so Jon would figure out a way to get it done. Doc, as Jon had come to call him, wanted him to do a recon mission to an android research facility which use to be a military base. It was nearby and only a short bus ride. Any venture, outside his building, was a danger to him. If he was captured now, it would mean the end of everything. Some things, though, just had to be done outside the world of the brains.

Doc had already done the research on the facility, so far as getting into the place. Jon made himself an identification card from information sent to him and put his geek clothes back on, then covered them with his janitor outfit. He would remove the coveralls on the last bus, after changing buses many times.

The guard saw exactly what he expected to see. A specialist who looked much too young and told him about something he needed to check which the guard nodded to intelligently but had no clue what the kid said. Armed with a visitors pass, Jon entered the facility and stopped at a floor plan posted on a wall in the lobby. He managed to get lost several times and once even bumped into a burly guard who just smiled at his buddy and directed Jon in the right direction. Jon mumbled his thanks and a long unnecessary apology as he walked away still talking to himself.

He managed to give himself a very thorough tour of the facility by the time he arrived at the place where he told everyone he needed to go. His task was a simple one, even if it had really needed to be performed. A single connection had somehow jarred loose. He could have fixed it with a pocket knife, he later told everyone he stumbled into on his way out.

He found one door guarded by four no nonsense guerrilla's in uniform.. He mumbled and apologized and showed them his visitors pass but they did not smile or move for him to enter through those doors.

"So, that must be where they keep them." He thought.

In a cavity of a room, Jon tapped on the keys of an unimportant work station. By going through various back doors of the facility's computer system, he soon found the security cameras of the section where the guards had no sense of humor. He looked at the monitor in amazement. The public, and Jon as well, were amazed with the progress in robotics. What Jon saw on the screen would make one think he had entered the future. Indeed, he had. He saw humans, no androids. He could not be sure. They sat patiently in chairs with computer cords running out their ears. Well, really out of various parts of their body. They were male and female, children and babies. Even some animals were seen in one corner.

Then, he saw something really amazing. One of the humans, working on an android, removed all the hook ups. The android got up from the chair and the human assumed the seated position. The android opened portals on the human and plugged in the computer cords. Jon realized his mouth was hanging open and that he was in a very dangerous place for him and had to get out without raising suspicion.

"Boy, did he have something to tell the Doc. Androids working on androids. Somewhere, someone had to be pushing some buttons. Didn't they?" He wondered as he left.

Verbally, he was mumbling and complaining about being sent to tighten a screw any nut with a screwdriver could have done. The people smiled at him. The guard smiled at him. Jon kept his slow rambling pace until he finally got out of sight of the gate guards.

On his return trip, he put his coveralls on, on the first bus and decided he was hungry. He would visit his mother before going back to his private dungeon with all its flashing, obsolete, computers. He knew now why the computer system had been left behind. Real technology had outgrown them.

The SUV with two blacksuits sat in an alley across the street. Jon went to his booth and waited for his waitress mother to come to the table. They went through the usual routine of pretending. He ordered a cheeseburger and received a plate of vegetables and milk instead of a soft drink. He smiled up at her. She smiled her best waitress smile and lingered at his table, pad and pencil in hand. She took a 'to go' order to the kitchen and returned to check on his drink. They had time for only snatches of chatter but he was able to assure her he was doing fine and that his work was very important.

He did not avoid the SUV but had started keeping his distance to avoid any possible recognition. One of the 'blacksuits' made a notation after he passed. Boy, did he have a lot to tell the Doc.

The blacksuits left when Jon's mother left to go home. They had to turn their reports in. It was just a matter of routine.

"Bill, Rick. Get in here!" A voice boomed from a private office marked "Section Chief" on the door.

The two men walked boldly in the office of Section Chief Broadman. Affectionately known as "Bubba' behind his back. Bubba was a square-faced giant of a man. He sat behind his desk like a kindergarten teacher trying to blend in with her class. Bubba looked up with disgust at the two men before him.

"Your report says you have been seeing a kid janitor at the diner." He said.

"Yes sir." They answered at the same time.

"Who is he?" Broadman asked.

"A janitor." Bill said a little to fast. Rick frowned.

"I did not ask what he did for a living. I asked who he is." Broadman schooled them out of the side of his mouth.

"We didn't ask, Sir." Rick replied. He wanted to back up a step but managed to stand where he was.

"A kid janitor visit's a diner and talks to the same waitress old enough to be his mother, for a month and you do not know his name." Broadman waited for a reply.

"We will find out, Sir." Bill assured him.

"Of course you will find out. You should have already found out. How would you two like to be uniformed guards on the subway?"

"Not at all." Rick replied.

"Never mind. Leave the boy alone. I'll take care of it. You two keep your same routine and take notes. It will be handled. You got me?" Broadman told them flatly.

"We got you Chief." Bill said.

Bubba waved them out and they were glad to leave.

"How is he going to handle it?" Rick wondered after they arrived in the locker room.

"Not a clue." Bill told him.

Jon brought some virtual coffee to Doctor Frank and Doctor Stein. They sat together. Jon had already told them his story. The human-android report both shocked and excited their whole group. They had gone off in two's and three's to discuss all the possibilities.

"These avatar characters are better than computer screens but I want to touch you and hold you." Doctor Frank told Ann.

"I know. Me too." Ann said.

"Those androids would give us human qualities with bodies that would outlast this age. We could have a part in a whole new future." Doctor Frank whispered.

"We could really be together."

"It would be a huge responsibility to inhabit a body like that. Artifical intelligence is one thing. Putting the essence of a human being inside a machine would advance even the ultra-modern world we have found." Ann reasoned.

"Yes. Yes, it would." Frank said. "It is the only way to find out the answers we need. We can only find a limited amount of information while in computer circuits. We never know if what we have discovered is a secret or just something they feed us to satisfy our curiosity."

"Whether, it works or not. I am for trying it." Ann said.

"Yes but we have to be very careful. We do not want to get lost somewhere in between the two existences. I believe the avatar program could be used as a false secondary existence to give the monitor guys something to watch while our essence is really in an android. We could back ourselves up someplace safe." Doctor Frank thought aloud.

"That might work. Yes. I think that would work." Ann

said.

"What?" Doctor Frank said, a bit startled. "Oh. Yes. I think it just might work."

"Did you forget I was here?" Ann asked.

"Never." He said with a smile.

"I know you Doctor Frank." She said, returning the smile.

"I love it when two brains come together." Jon said from beside their table, causing both of them to jump.

"Jon. We have a tentative plan." Ann told him.

"Great. I like tentative." Jon said.

All three smiled. They owed Jon a lot and both knew they would never be able to repay him fully.

"I've got a surprise for you Ann." She raised an eyebrow.

"Look through those trees over there to the right. See that little cabin." She nodded. "That's ours. We are going to spend the night here."

She squeezed his hands in hers. "That's wonderful."

Jon's avatar blushed down to his collar.

"It will get our monitor techs used to us staying here. They will find it fascinating." Doctor Frank said.

Now that the big brains had decided on a plan, Jon had to get back to his computer banks and work out some of the details. He watched Doctor Frank and Doctor Stein until they walked hand-in-hand across a little bridge. He got a glimpse of something different. Well, he had not noticed the cabin either. "So what." He thought. Still there was something.

Jon went for his daily meal. It had all become routine now. He would order a burger of some sort and his mother would bring him a healthy meal. Today would be no different.

They chatted a little while she pretended to write. No she really was writing. Jon watched her.

"How do you like your job?" His mother asked.

"Fine. Thank you." He replied.

"That's good." His mother said.

"I ain't had a better one." Jon said. He did not know

why he used the word his mother always corrected him on. It was just part of his instinct kicking in. He had been tricked and scammed on computers, so he had a natural defense mechanism. He let it pass when she did not correct him. Even his mother could slip once in a while. She came now with his plate of veggies he had come to enjoy. They seemed to give him longer lasting energy. It was not veggies on the plate. There was the burger and fries he had jokingly ordered. His mother smiled as she placed them on the table.

"Thank you very much." Jon said.

"You are welcome." She said looking all around instead of directly into his eyes as she always did when speaking to him.

Jon did not know why but he thought of the room of androids he had seen at the facility. Those human looking androids. He looked around the diner at the cook and the other waitresses. No one seemed to pay attention to him.

"Well Marge, I have to go back to work." Jon told his mother.

She did not notice the first name. He always called her mother.

Jon ordered a take-out and left in his usual manner. Something was horribly wrong. What had happened to his mother? He feared he would be followed but he arrived alone.

Broadman questioned the supervisor at the android detection department.

"No. It is not him." The voice said. "He called her Marge."

"What did he order?" Broadman asked.

"Just a burger and fries." The voice said.

"What did Marge serve him." Broadman asked.

"Why are you interrogating me? She served him what he asked for!"

"His mother would not give him a burger! He somehow figured out that the waitress was an android. Didn't you have a mama?" Broadman yelled as he hung up the phone.

He dialed Bill and Rick in their SUV. "He is on to us."

"How do you know?" Someone asked then regretted it.

"Never mind. Just pick up the janitor next time you see him and leave his mother alone." Broadman hung up before they could respond. He liked doing that.

Jon did not go back to the diner. He found a little place in the opposite direction and ordered something to go from then on. Sometimes, he'd order enough for a couple of days and heat it up. Man! He missed his vegetables and his mother. He missed her a lot now.

He did not fail to take precautions though. He ditched his janitor's outfit. It seems his office building held a lot of unfound treasure. He took some time off and ventured some of the office suites, gladly finding a shower that worked and a suit of clothes that fit him. He looked pretty good, he decided, even with his tennis shoes.

Meanwhile, his mother was stuck at home again. She had been unceremoniously fired from the little diner without being given a reason. When she made a phone call, she heard minute noises in the background and a black SUV was always parked someplace on her street. Her backyard was fenced, so she could not make an exit that way, without making a spectical of herself.

She decided to call her little sister Rachel. She was a spunky little thing about her size but with rich blonde hair straight out of a bottle.

She told Rach her plan to which she responded with excited giggles. She never did outgrow those. Marge found an old wig she use to wear back when her and her sister had tried to pass for twins. They had fooled a good number of people.

Marge got Rachel to walk around the house some so she could learn to imitate her bouncy walk. She had a way of always looking carefree even when she was not so happy. They swapped clothes and Marge was off in Rach's car. She drove to the mall and a couple of other places before going into the district where Jon's office building was located. She found a diner in the area and sipped on a diet soft drink while she waited. It was about time for Jon to be hungry again. She was not disappointed. Jon saw her and came in. His very first impulse was to ask his aunt why she was in that part of town. Then he saw that it was his mother. She gently motioned for him to sit across from her.

The waitress came over and took Jon's order. Then, Jon and the pretty blonde smiled at each other.

"You make a pretty blonde." Jon said.

"My name is Rachel and you." Marge said.

He followed her lead and introduced himself. Jon enjoyed his meal but he enjoyed the part his mother was playing even more. She made a point of flirting with Jon every time the waitress got within earshot. They were both careful to remember that someone could be listening.

After a convincing time of patting hands and laughing, they left the diner together. They held hands, laughed and whispered to each other all along the maze-like route Jon took back to the office building. Once they were safely inside the building, Jon gave his mother the hug he had been wanting to give her since the first night in the diner. He told her everything. She listened wide-eyed as he told her of the brains, the avatars, and the complicated plans they were trying to work out.

She agreed with what he was doing but expressed fear for his safety. Then, she decided to help him. Whatever the cost, she would help her son free these people from their prison. It was the right thing to do. She would do as Jon had done, disappear until it was all over. She would go back home and she and Rachel would work out a plan, then she would come to help Jon. There was an underground parking garage for her car.

Jon walked her back to the diner to get her car, then he was back and bent over his computer trying to work out some

details. The night passed without him being aware. There were a few things he had to talk to Doctor Frank about.

Chapter Five

Jon checked into their virtual world. The population had grown tremendously. Reverend Dewey Wright had already erected a little church on one of the hills. People were absolutely swarming all over the place. Jon, with apron on, served coffee and tea to his patrons. If only this was a real world café, he could be rich. People played their parts very well, pretending to drink their coffee and tea.

Doctor Frank and Doctor Stein came down the walk from their new virtual home. They seemed to have adapted to this new world and were enjoying their time together. They even held hands most of the time.

Jon met them outside and took a break with them under a gazebo. The others left them to talk. Jon caught a movement that seemed out of the ordinary but it was gone now. He could not put his finger on it but something was not right.

"We cannot transfer your essences to the androids. It is much too dangerous. Oh, we can do the transfer okay, but if you were discovered, all they would have to do is sever the link with your brain. You would have only the programming that was uploaded with no human input after that." Jon explained.

"Yes." Doctor Frank said. "I had not thought of that. What are our other options?"

"I've been working on that." Ann sat wide-eyed looking from one to the other. "We can transfer the brains, your brains, into an android shell complete with cerebrospinal fluid. You would be in complete control of the android. The android would be you." Jon waited. He could almost hear the wheels turning in the doctor's head.

"You know of such android shells?" Doctor Frank asked.

"I do. They are in a very secure part of the facility I visited. We will have to work out a very sophisticated heist to get them out. My plan is not complete but instead of breaking in to get them, I thought we would just let them walk out." Jon paused while they looked at him with questions on their face.

"How?" Ann asked.

"Exactly." Doctor Frank said looking at Ann then Jon.

"I think I can program them just enough to get them out. I'll have to do some serious hacking, maybe from the inside. Getting your brains into them is another problem. I'd rather not do it in their present location because there will be a period of adjustment. Of course, if we did load them at the brain trust, we could continue the program to get them to bring you to the office building. The only problem is how to do the transfer and who will do it." Jon stopped then.

"Well, I have an idea." Frank said.

"You can program a dozen android shells as well as you can program a couple. Right?" Doctor Frank said and asked.

"Yes, of course." Jon replied.

"Good. We make it look like a general uprising of the androids. The technician androids will, most likely, not be programmed for that eventuality, so they should not be a problem. We'll need some to take out the guards temporarily. Upload a martial arts program to them. Also, fix it so they respond only to your commands. You can direct them to the office and they can escort our shells." Doctor Frank was explaining as he mapped out the plan in his head.

"Okay." Jon agreed.

"We will need a couple of the active androids uploaded with the necessary skills to make the transfer. They may already have that ability." Doctor Frank said.

"That still leaves the problem of getting your brains, you, this is confusing, out of the brain trust and to the office building." Jon said.

Ann broke her silence. "A medical emergency would work. We get them in transport to the biological repair facility and detour them. Reprogrammed android drivers would work for that."

Jon scratched his head. They were talking out the details of the plan. He was seeing various program conversions of the same plans.

"I'll need help. My Mom and aunt are as good as I am with computers. I'm a better hacker but once I get them inside, they can do the work. I'll talk to them." Jon said.

Doctor Frank and Ann had their work cut out for them as well. They would have to deal with the other brains and convince them to take on their vitals until they were in the clear. That way, no alarms would be set off.

They had to meet with the other brains in the other virtual world that had been set up by the trust. They'd have to do some busy work to occupy the levels above them. Doctor Banks would have to be contacted and filled in on their plans. A list must be made of those who wanted to leave with them and those who wanted to stay. They would have to be careful that their plan was not exposed. So, only necessary information would be disseminated. They would tell the 'what' but not the 'how' of the plan.

There must be a thousand things to do before this plan came together but what was that to brains already several hundred years old. They would make it work.

Ann worked up a hundred or so pages of a book she had planned to write someday. She would set the program to upload a few pages a day after they made their escape. Doctor Frank worked on some equations that meant little but would keep some mathematics professors busy trying to figure them out. He also made the upload progressive.

Doctor Trey Banks, from the third level, had been busy. He contacted Doctor Frank and Doctor Stein to arrange a meeting. Although the members were scattered through several levels, they managed to set up a conference and to include Jon.

"Doctor Banks, you have something to tell us." Doctor Frank stated.

"Yes. I'm afraid it is a rather long statement. Good Morning everyone. Or what ever the time." He said the last under his breath which brought a smile to all their faces. "I have conducted an investigation of our situation. One thing I did is disguise my assistant and close friend David in a Pest Control Technician uniform and send him out to spray for bugs. We used only environmentally friendly mix."

Again, a smile. They were all very much dependent on their environment. "Since few people notice workers of that class, he was able to venture far and wide. His report is being downloaded to your screens as I speak."

He continued. "Finally, we have a broad view of our situation. Of course, the report is limited by the amount of area David was able to cover. After roaming freely for some time, he was rudely acousted at level ten and turned back. He did find out that we are in a cone shaped, well organized facility. Each level is progressive in nature. By that I mean, each level represents the technology advances of that era. David saw computer systems even he did not understand just by observation. Although, I'm sure if he got his hands on them, he would figure them out. The cone shape represents the beginning with Doctor Frank at the bottom tip surrounded by those of his generation. It progresses in ever wider circles from there forming a cone.

"Now, outside this cone of intellectuals are tunnels of administrative and maintenance areas all supporting the cone area in some manner. Apparently, as the rows of highly intelligent brains were installed (for lack of a better word), there was more and more need for support. Therefore, brains were recruited from all sections of society. As you can imagine, the complexity of this facility is enormous."

Doctor Banks paused to allow anyone who had a thought to interject. Doctor Frank was drawing on a piece of paper. At least, it appeared to be paper. He drew an upside-down cone with the corridors leding off from every level. Then he put a huge 'X' at the bottom.

"What have I done?" He said aloud.

"You could not have known Doctor." Banks assured him.

"I should have known. Frank replied.

"As we suspected, someplace, someone is draining off brain power to use in every facet of society, or so we think. I believe, and I hope someone proves me wrong, that our brains are no longer an experiment but have become the cornerstone of society. In other words, the world revolves around the brain complex."

"How far out does our world go before you find a real world?" It was Mike, Doctor Stein's assistant, who spoke.

"Our investigation did not reveal that." Doctor Banks told the group. "The inner core where the brains are is very real, of course, but within the confines of all the computer networks are, seemingly, endless virtual worlds. You may escape a virtual world to a real world, only to find out later that the real world you escaped to is another layer of virtual reality." Doctor Banks paused again.

Doctor Stein had been silent but now she spoke. "Yes. Yes it would have to be so. With minds like these, they would never accept that there world was all that existed. So, they would be given a window of escape. The window would be difficult and many would not find it but for those who did it would seem that they were free of their bonds."

Jon added. "But in reality, they are still where they were, only their minds work and play in a different virtual world."

"I'm sure there are some airplanes crashing someplace. This discussion has filled up every corner of my brain and

I'm still confused." Doctor Frank admitted.

"I understand how you feel Doctor, but I'm sure you are mistaken. We freely use only a part of our brains. The rest is used for purposes beyond our ability to understand. Or so they say. Who ever 'they are. I think they mean beyond our awareness." Doctor Banks said.

"Well, I promise you all. I will find out just how far this thing goes. They designed this system based on my theories. You can be sure there is a key someplace and I intend to find it." Doctor Frank said.

"That's my husband!" Doctor Stein exclaimed.

"I expect you all have visualized where we are by now. Doctor Frank, I see you have drawn it out on paper. Well, if you notice the drawing, the cone leaves a space in the middle, with the cone filled with brains, cascading upward around the vacate center." Doctor Banks again paused.

"I got a feeling that you've been saving something Doctor." Mike said.

"Indeed, I have. There could not exist such a complex system without control. No group of technicians, sitting at wherever the top is located, could keep all these magnificent minds in harmony. It would have to be done by an equally brilliant mind using its full capacity. Suspended in the center of this complex is a single brain. David got a glimpse of it from the tenth level. It was far in the distance. Extended from the brain in all directions, to every level were connections like tentacles reaching out. We think this brain provides the kind of continuity necessary to keep order and purpose. The big question, as I see it, is who is this brain and can we make contact. Then, can we persuade him or her to come over to our side." Doctor Banks said.

"That brain must have some stories to tell." Mike mused.

"So, am I in a virtual world or the real thing?" Jon asked.

"We don't know. You may have broken through all the virtual layers since you used Doctor Frank's back door to get in." Banks tried to reassure him.

"Well, in that case, I'll just have to see if that brain up there has a back door. You folks take care. I have work to do." With that Jon left the meeting.

They were all exhausted and so closed their discussion until another appointed time. There was a lot to think about. The big question now was would their planned escape get them out of the virtual maze or just into another layer of what was fast becoming a virtual world of madness.

"Honey, let's go home." Ann said. They had started calling their avatar home, home. For just a little while, they could pretend it was all real.

"I'd like that. Maybe we can go for a walk down by the creek." Doctor Frank said.

"See you there."

"See ya."

Jon kicked back in his chair. He thought briefly of his room at home with his two computers, hooked up to two brains. In the world he lived in, those were two very powerful computers. He could actually carry on a conversation with those two brains or he could just type away and let the information flow.

Marge and Rachel were working on the android project. Later, he would tell them about his meeting. Right now, he wished for the personal relationships he had with his computers at home. He had programmed in shortcuts and such that saved him a lot of time. He had long ago installed a server so that space was never a problem. Still, he had made himself at home with the rows of computers he now controlled. He assumed he controlled them. Everything was so uncertain since his meeting with the brains. "Okay Jon." He told himself. "You have to work with the assumption that this is the real world. You have to work toward a solution as if it were going to happen, when and if all the details are worked out."

"I'm hungry." He announced.

"So am I." Echoed Marge and Rachel.

They were off to the diner. They decided it would be best to drive. Jon smeared a little mud on the bulb over the license plate to make it less easy to read but not so much that they would get pulled over for the light being out. It was a given that, by now, they were on all the important watch list.

"We have to make other arrangements." Marge said.

"Yeah, they got to be watching for us." Rachel chimmed in.

"Mom, you could open a little clothing shop in the building. We could block it off. I'm sure Doctor Frank would set you up. That way, you two could take turns keeping it open. Then, we could order takeout without attracting attention." Jon concluded.

"Sounds good to me." Marge agreed.

"The added benefit would be that we could have more than one change of clothes, too." Rachel said.

They were at the drive thru now and started calling out their order to the speaker. Marge was driving. Just as they were getting their change from the girl at the window, a black SUV pulled up in the lane behind them. The two men inside seemed to be looking at the menu instead of them.

Just as they thought they were home free. One of the men pointed in their direction. The chase was now on. Marge wasted no time in getting onto the street and heading toward the city and away from their office building. She was making a turn onto a side street as the SUV pulled out in pursuit. They saw the SUV through an alleyway as they headed in the opposite direction. Marge again took a side street heading further away from the SUV. She took them on a whirlwind ride through a mall and a junk yard. As the other looked at her in surprise, she smiled.

"I've been studying the city map." Marge explained.

Marge hit the turnpike heading in the general direction of the office building. There was no sighting of the SUV. Quickly, before the men in the SUV could call for backup, she turned off the turnpike and sprinted for the office building. Jon hit the ground at a run as she slid to a halt outside the door to the parking area. In a moment, they were inside and Jon had the door down.

Laughing together as they headed toward their underground work area, Rachel commented. "That was fun."

"You'd think so." Marge teased her. She was still laughing.

"Well, we can't let that happen again." Jon said seriously. "I have to admit though, I was proud of you Mom."

To his dismay, she just messed his hair and smiled at him.

Doctor Frank and the love of his life walked quietly by the stream. It was a long time before anyone spoke. Ann turned to him, stopping him in his tracks. He looked into her eyes and saw that she was troubled.

"What is it my dear?" He asked.

"You noticed?" Ann asked.

"Yes. I noticed. He said.

"I've been having dreams." She said.

"That's normal enough, given the circumstances." He replied. "What are they about, some adventure to unknown planets or a firefight between aircraft?" He realized as soon as he said it that he had spoken too lightly. She did not smile.

"No. Nothing like that. I have dreams of thousands of voices speaking to me and me speaking back. We talk of making the world a better place, families, Oh, lots of stuff. It's not really conversation. It is more like flashes of communication but not conversation. Does that make sense?" Ann asked.

"You are not aware of these 'thoughts' during your waking hours?" He asked.

"No not so much. Sometimes, maybe, there are flashes. In those cases, my mind seems to respond without any thought on my part and the flash is gone. Weird. Right?" She asked.

"That depends on how you describe weird. Our whole

situation is starting to seem a little weird, even if I did sort of mastermind the whole thing." He said.

"Sort of! Without you, it would not exist!" She said with more feeling that she usually expressed.

"So, my genius, what is the answer?" She asked. A lot calmer now.

"I want you to concentrate more on the flashes. If you block out your daily activities, you may get a much clearer picture of what ever is or is not going on in your subconscious." He said.

"Okay. I'll try. I wanted to rest awhile before time for bed anyway and you have some genius work to do." The last part teasing.

He did have a lot of work to do. Jon could not do it all. He also wanted to visit Reverend Wright again.

Chapter Six

It was the most powerful position in the world. There was no glory attached to the exalted standing. Bright lights illuminated toward it and a pulsating white glow radiated out, penetrating the depths and the heights surrounding it.

The Brain was fully shielded from outside forces. It was aware of world events but immune to being force fed information. The curiosity of the Brain kept it hungry for details from innumerable sources.

A series of protective measures, inacted by the Brain itself, kept it secure from sabotage. The brain controlled fluid intake when needed and other maintenance functions.

Originally, technicians monitored vitals and emotional changes of the brain. That was long ago. The Brain had taken over these duties and was much more qualified to do so.

In short, the Brain had been installed as a tool but had progressed to the point where the installers were the tools. That is IF they had been still alive. The Brain had outlived them all. Its accumulated knowledge, through the centuries, made it the obvious choice to look after itself. With all the protections put in place, no change could be made without the Brain, even if it had been logical to do so.

It was not ego. It was only logical that the most intellectually advanced make these decisions. The Brain looked outside itself with a bit of wonder. It could do so through millions of digital images flashed to its receptors. Better than having actual eyes, for nothing was missed. There were no eyes for the array of bright lights to damage. The tentacles ran from the clear pod, that enclosed itself, reaching beyond reach of a human eye. Every square pixel was known to the Brain. Every brain, aware of the presence of the shining one at the center of the complex. Soothing thoughts entered the brains at appropriate times of stress. There was mutual and genuine affection between them.

Ann relaxed on the soft bed of their virtual home. She put aside the days activities and the problems. She drifted into the comfortable space between waking and sleeping.

Then, she began to search. She wanted to drift into the hidden compartments of her mind. In some of those compartments, there was pain and disappointment. She had put them there to avoid being distracted by them. It was there that she placed her own ambitions when she fell in love with her husband. His dreams became her dreams and so her dreams were put aside. She was not sorry.

It became as if she were knocking on doors as she relaxed. Some opened easy enough, others were stubbornly locked to her. Even in her slumber, this irritated her. It was, after all, her mind. If any one had a right to look behind those doors, it was her. She could not accept secrets being kept from her in her own mind. She would not accept that.

In her mind, she forced a door open that did not want to move. There were frightening sights inside and she quickly shut the door. Those were the fears that she had conquered long ago. Better to keep them locked up. Another door pushed open. Inside were her childhood memories. The swing in the backyard held a laughing little girl. A voice called to the little girl and she ran bouncingly toward the kitchen door. Ann remembered that day now.

Another closed door, or almost one open only slightly,

opened easily under her touch. Yes. She remembered. Behind this door were her religious beliefs that she once held so dear to her heart. Reluctantly, she turned back to the corridor and the door at the end.

Down this corridor of her mind she slowly walked. Her steps carried her ever closer to a door with light emanating through every crack around the door. Should she dare to open that door?

Her hands slid along other doors that were closed to her but she was not concerned with them now. That door with the light was drawing her. Her hand reached out to touch it.

"Ann! Ann! Wake up Ann!" It was Doctor Frank.

"Oh. Hello honey. I must have dropped off." Ann said.

"Dropped off! You were asleep for four hours!." He told her.

"Four hours!" She sat up in bed.

"I would have let you sleep but you were talking in your sleep. Something about a light." He said.

"Yes. Light and there was a door. I was going toward a door with light streaming out all around it. It was beautiful." Ann said, a little too dreamy.

"Come. We will sit by the fire and drink some hot chocolate before we get back to bed." Doctor Frank said. He wanted her head to clear before she went back to sleep.

"I did it. I broke into my subconscience. It was like a corridor with doors opening off it. Some opened easily while others refused to open. I forced one open and it was very scary inside." Ann told him. "I don't remember having those thoughts.

"The subconscious holds many secrets." He said.

"The door with the light seemed to draw me, to call to me." She left him then, her eyes searching the flames of the fire.

"Ann?" He asked with concern.

"I'm so sorry. Honey. What does it mean? Are the answers

Preserved Intellect & Harvest 2050AD   Milton J Southerland

we seek behind that mysterious door? I'm so consfused." She
let herself be helpless with him for the first time. She wanted
him to search his brillant mind and give her an answer. He
wanted to help her but no answer came. He just held her
lifeless avatar. Ann drifted off to sleep there by the fire.
Doctor Frank
slipped out quietly to visit with Reverend Wright. It could tell
from the sound effects that it would have been a cold night in
the virtual world. Had it not been virtual, that is.

Reverend Wright sat on the step at the front of his little
church. He appeared to be deep in thought. Doctor Frank
stood at the door, hesitating to go in.

"Come in Doctor." Dewey's voice boomed even when he
was trying to talk softly.

"How are you Reverend?" Doctor Frank asked.

"Call me Dewey." He said.

"Okay."

"What's on your mind?" The preacher asked.

"Funny question." Doctor Frank said with a half smile.

"Old habit."

"It is my wife. She seems near a breakdown of some sort. I
saw it, many years ago, in patients who later slipped into a
comma. Bad thing, those commas. The person is there but
there is no two way communication. It is as if they are all
alone in their own mind." Doctor Frank said.

"Very sad state to be in." Dewey said.

"You've seen it." Doctor Frank asked.

"Oh yes. I reckon I have seen about every sad state a
human can get in. If I did not see it myself, I have heard
the story through sobs and tears which make a story very
real."

"I suppose it does."

"I made a mistake. I wanted her to explore some
unexplained flashes she was experiencing. She has a very
strong mind. I thought she might find some answers to our
problems. You see there is a brain being used as a central

71

guide to the rest of us. We appear to have freedom of thought but it is the part of our brain that 'they' are using that the central guide helps." Dewey listened intently. "It provides emotional support
and continuity of purpose."

"Yes. They would need a setup like that." Dewey said.

"I never foreseen the project growing to such an extent and therefore did not predict the need for such a setup." Doctor Frank said.

"You had no way of knowing." The preacher assured him.

"I should have." Doctor Frank said.

"You are not responsible for what other people did after you were out of control of the project." Dewey said.

"I suppose it could be looked at like that but I am not a freshman in college. I should have known. Now, it is pulling, the only person I ever loved, away from me. If I only had hands I would fight it."

"It was your mind that built it. Fight with your mind."

"Of course. My mind. I must use what I have."

Ann's avatar was gone. Doctor Frank searched the area, the stream where they walked, the diner. She was gone. He went back to his other world and got hold of her assistant.

"Mike, have you seen or talked to Doctor Stein." He asked.

"No Doctor. Her work station is gone. Just the office shell is still there." Mike said.

He contacted the third level. Doctor Banks had not heard from her. She had simply disappeared.

"Doctor Banks. What about her actual brain? Is it still in place?" Doctor Frank asked.

"No. Turns out, what we were seeing was a program which had apparently been set up for our benefit. All the stuff that has been going on was real but routed from another location. At least, that is the best scenrio I can come up with." He said.

"Thank you Doctor."

"You are welcome."

There was nothing more for the two men to say. Doctor

Frank's emotions spiked and he was suddenly very sleepy. They would sedate his brain. He played along and went 'home' to bed.

Jon, in the meantime, was going ahead with the program. He was not yet aware of Ann's disappearance. He had decided that stealing a dozen or two androids would cause quite a stir, so he decided to purchase some empty ones and a half dozen or so to use as guards. He could change their loyalty algorithm to take input only from himself and his crew.

Money was not a problem. Doctor Frank had allowed him access to his financial empire which was considerable. A few hundred years interest adds up. As for delivery, he would rent a truck and bring them in himself. No reason to give the enemy their location.

"That is a good plan." Marge told her son proudly.

"Well, I just hope it works." Jon said.

Rachel was up front in the store doing a thriving business. She reported having more than two customers already.

"How many more?" Marge had asked.

"One more. We've had three customers. All looked just like regular shoppers to me." She added.

Jon took a rare break and flipped on the television. The news people seemed all in a tizzy. They jumped from story to story as fast as they could get the reporters up on satelite. Even with the skies full of orbiting junk, there was still a few seconds delay.

The Defense Department spokesman was livid. They would find the terrorist who were messing with their brain system. Pilots were having to fly their own planes and manually set attack patterns.

The weather service was calling in all the forecasters, long since laid off. Some were already drawing retirement. Some were dead. In their wisdom, they had shut down training programs for meterologist.

The elevators to one of the orbiting tourist attractions had stalled somewhere above the cloud cover. No shuttles were going up due to a computer system that had suddenly turned very emotional.

"Did you say emotional?" The reporter asked someone.

"Well, for lack of a better word. Yes." The man said.

"Are you hinting that it is acting like a woman?"

"Of course not. Men have emotions too. Why are we even discussing this on the air anyway?"

"Does it bother you to talk about it?" The reporter persisted.

Jon laughed and changed the channel. Asia was no better. He did not understand the language but the pictures were the same. A nuclear reactor had decided to vent some radiation all by itself which forced an emergency evacuation of a few thousand people.

Marge came up to stand beside Jon. "I read about things like this happening in history. Those were caotic times." She said.

"Looks like those days are back. I wonder what has the brains all discombobulated. It is the brains, you know." Jon told her.

"Yes. I'm sure. We just wanted to get a couple of people together and now look what's happening." She said.

"Well. It was bound to happen anyway. You cannot use people's brains for hundreds of years and expect them to never wake up. I think they have paid their dues. The government is getting just what it had coming to it."

"But the people?" Marge questioned.

"Which people? The ones in the containers or those out there," he waved his hand toward the television, "living in ease because of the overworked brains."

"I see what you mean. You are wise beyond your years." She said.

"I will have to get a lot wiser soon. I have to get inside the central brain and find out what is going on." He said. "Otherwise, these people will blow each other up. Mom, would you order the androids while I search for back door access to the central brain. This is not fun anymore." The last was spoken as he turned to his keyboard. Marge laid a hand on his shoulder and went to her own task. A tear slipped from one eye. "He has too much on him for such a young man." She thought.

Broadman kicked his desk and shoved the files, on his desk, into the floor. Bill and Rick stepped back a step as if they were attached, to each other. Their beepers went off, but there was no message. It was just a bunch of programmer language which none of them remotely understood. They replaced them on their belts and the batteries were suddenly hot. They smelled smoldering cloth. It was the waistband of their trousers.

Broadman pulled his off and tossed it in the trash. Bill and Rick pulled theirs off their belt but not know-ing what to do with them, they tossed them from one hand to the other.

"Put them in the trash, you idiots." Broadman yelled.

"Thank you chief." Rick said. Bill elbowed him.

"You know…we live in the most technologically advanced age in the history of the world. We have more information at our fingertips than at any other time. The problem is that the cops I have to work with are getting more stupid by the minute." Broadman lectured.

"Us too Boss?" Rick asked.

"No, of course not. Where is that kid?" he asked

sarcastically.

"They don't eat no more Boss." Rick was doing most of the talking and digging a hole big enough for him and his partner. Bill knew it too.

"Of course, they eat. The kid was eating the last time you saw him. That means he is not an android. So if he was eating before, he must still be eating. The question is: Where is he getting the food? The other question is: Who was that with him? The other question is: Have you checked to see if his mother is at home. The other question is: Why are you still standing in my office?"

"I don't know why Boss." Rick said. Bill pulled him from the office by a handful of coat.

Doctor Frank laid in his bed. He let his mind relax. It was the same as he told Ann to do before she left him. He let his thoughts drift away from all the formulas and calculations that were always in his mind. Even when he was talking to Ann or in a meeting, those numbers and theories were always there as he tried to unravel some mystery.

Now, he pushed those things aside. He saw himself floating in the comforting cerebrospinal fluid that he knew surrounded his brain. He traveled through the cortical centers searching for the door that would show him the way to his lost love.

The technician monitoring him saw a dramatic change and notified Doctor Banks. He was advised to let the doctor alone so long as he was stable.

"Good luck Doctor Frank." He said to himself. "I hope you find her."

Doctor Frank was amazed when he entered the parietal lobe of his cerebrum. The part of the brain that, at one time, communicated with the body giving such signals as touch and pain through somatosensory input. There was no need for this communication now, for there was no body to communicate with. The amazing part, he found, was the adaptability of the brain. This part of his brain had found new purpose in communicating with signals from the fluid the brain itself floated in.

Although amazing, it was not the area Doctor Frank sought. He was seeking a mysterious region of the diencephalons located between the prethalamus and thalamus. It was called zona limitans intrathalamiea. Located just north of the spinal cord, it was a signaling center for the brain. Doctor Frank had a signal to send.

Chapter Seven

On a rocky hillside, in the shadow of the great mountains, a cavern of immense size left a gaping hole like the mouth of a monster.

A well traveled trail led into the mountain, carved by centuries of bare feet, shoed feet and various objects being dragged along behind a hunter. A gate made of saplings was pushed aside, to be closed when the sun went down.

Walking down the trail into the great cavern, we find torches lighting our way, providing a dim view of the way ahead. Some very old artifacts crumpled slowly along the walls. Here and there animal hides cure, stretched tightly toward the edges of hand-crafted frames. The smell is a little musky but with the odor of fire smoke and animal fat cooking. The ceilings are high above, beyond the dim light of the torches. Each step leaves a whisper of sound echoing upward into the far reaches of somewhere.

In a curtained off room, the curtain is pulled back, two men sit beside a fire pit that has been vented into the dark reaches above. No doubt, there is a hole up there to let the smoke escape.

The two men, one very old the other a young man, gaze into the flames. The old man rocks gently in a rocker made of curved saplings. An animal hide makes do for a cushion. We seem to have walked into the past, the opposite is true. Mirrors of metal from some bygone era reflected light from the torches and fire so that the old man is able to read his books quite comfortably. Indeed, he choose the spot for that very reason. He has spent his life pouring over the many books stored in a vault with hard rock walls. A table sets against the wall where he has transcribed copies of many of the books which he passed on to other historians, some from far away places, some he will never see again.

"Grandfather, tell me again of what it was like before the days of darkness." The voice is booming for a young man, magnified by the cavern walls.

"You could tell the story as well as I. You read almost as much as me. Were it not for your farming, I fear you would never stop reading." Grandfather said. His voice alternated from a deep baritone to a little squeaky until he cleared his throat and continued.

Grandfather's appearance was weathered. The top of his head reflected the light of the fire because of baldness. Gray hair hung down around the edges almost to his collar. His large ears poked through the strands of hair. He was bundled against the dampness with the hide of an elk, given to him by the grandson who now talked with him. His name was Bradley although few used that name. He was just Grand-father to the other adults and the children that he spoiled endlessly.

"You should be with that sweetheart of yours, not sitting here talking to an old man." Grandfather said.

"She ran me off. She was going down to the falls to bathe." The young man said. Grandfather nodded. Already, she was helping on the vegetable farm and seemed to love the work.

The young man was not as tall as Grandfather but he had the muscles of someone who had known nothing but work since childhood. He had taken some land and prepared the soil for farming by the time he was a dozen years old. Then, he was providing fresh vegetables for the clan by the time he was thirteen. He was a skilled hunter but understood, better than many, the importance of eating fresh vegetables along with meat. He was called Ben for Benjamin, from an ancient book. It was said that Benjamin was loved and so the name fit his grandson well for he was loved by most everyone. He just had that way about him.

"There was a time when the wilderness had been tamed and people had made great machines to help them in their work." Grandfather could tell a story. It was more fun than reading, well for most anyway. The skies had streaks of ice where the flying machines, called airplanes, soared high in the blue. There are tales of men going beyond our atmosphere into the very heavens.

"It is recorded in the books how many kingdoms fall into ruin but none so great as the fall of the kingdom of the flying time." His voice shrieked slightly and he cleared his throat and calmed his thoughts.

"They were adrift in knowledge and technology. They were torn between using it for good and domination. In a very old book, I have found stories of legendary characters who lived even before the flying time, whether real or not, who reached great heights of learning. They also failed in their struggle between helping their fellow man or ruling them. The people of the flying time had every opportunity to learn from history. Yet, they stumbled or ran into the same pit of destruction.

"Look around you boy. See the remains of a great civilization. Look beyond the forest to the shore of the great oceans. Look to the bottom of the sea. You will see what remains of the greatest technologically inclined minds in history. Still, they could not balance their advances with the emotions that boiled within their soul.

"Our home, this very structure was built for the day when they would destroy each other. They expected it to happen, still they blundered on. Their weapons advancing beyond their restraint, until there was no path back. They developed ways to see in the dark but forgot the darkness of men's souls. They built machines that surprised even them with their abilities and complexity. They developed images of themselves so that their thoughts might exist beyond the durability of their own flesh."

Grandfather started to rise from his chair but sat back down hard.

"You need to rest now Grandfather." Ben told him. "I will get you some tea."

Ben retrieved a spoon of tea and dumped it into a cup. He poured water from the pot near the fire. Grandfather had gone to sleep. No doubt, his great mind was visiting the places he had read about or perhaps he soared over the land and looked for clues of the past. Ben let him sleep as he leaned back, stirring the tea as he thought on the words he had heard.

Grandfather awoke, clearing his throat and grumbling something about being too old to stay awake long enough to tell a story.

Ben scooped out the tea leaves and handed the cup to his beloved grandfather. It was time to sit quietly now. He had much to consider. Perhaps, someday it would be up to him to tell the stories to the next generation.

Hannah went past the door slinging water from her long brown hair. She guessed Ben saw her but did not look his way. She sang a little song which he could hear but not make out the words. He knew the tune though. It was something Hannah hummed when she was happy, which was about all the time.

"Grandfather" Ben said.

"Yes Grandson."

"I wonder if I could spend some time in your library? The crops are plowed and weeded. They will keep for a week or so." Ben told him.

"A week or so. You planning on reading the whole library?" Grandfather asked with a twinkle.

"No. It's not that. I just want to read some of the books I've been skipping over. You know manuals and stuff." Ben said.

"You mean the boring stuff."

"You remember. That was what I said ten years ago when you first took me inside." Ben replied.

"Sure. Just handle the books gently. You know they are very old. Some of them could be the only copies in existence."

"Yes sir. I know. Someday, I'd like to start copying some for you." Ben said.

"The sooner, the better." Grandfather told him.

Ben got up to leave the room and check on Hannah. He needed to tell her where he would be for a few days. He found her in the kitchen. Her skin all aglow and a smile at his appearance. She continued to hum the tune she was humming when he came into the room. He told her his plans, to which, she did not object.

"I'll keep an eye on the fields." She volunteered.

"Thank you." He said and was off to the library.

He walked to the technical manuals section and picked up a few before he found one that intrigued him. It was a dusty manual on something called electricity. The manual took his attention away. It was his stomach that reminded him that he had not eaten since breakfast. He walked to the kitchen and found a kettle still warm on the stove. Inside was a stew made from last years crop and flavored with packaged seasoning. He consumed a good portion. Looking up from his bowl, he say Hannah propped in the doorway watching him eat.

"You eat like you were gone a week." She teased.

"It seems like it." He replied.

"Find anything interesting?" She asked.

"Lots of stuff. I have to get back." He said getting up.

"Tonight." She wondered.

"I need to study some diagrams while they are fresh on my mind." He said.

"I understand. I'm going to bed. I'll see you in the morning?" She asked.

"Of course, we always go to the spring together."

"Very well. Goodnight then." She stretched for a kiss

and giggled when he persisted. She pushed away then told him. "You have things to learn. Remember?"

"I sure do. Good thing for you, too."

"O yeah!" She said. "We will be married soon." Then she ran off to her room.

Ben headed for the library and his manuals. It was morning when he put them down. He had drawn out a diagram from the book which showed how to make something called an electric generator. It was always windy up on the mountain so turning the device would not be a problem. Or perhaps, the waterfall would work. He ask Grandfather.

"The waterfalls for sure. You would need less wire and the shorter distance might be better." He said.

"Grandfather, why has no one thought of building an electric generator before?" Ben asked.

"I'm sure they have Grandson."

"Then why?"

"I expect it is fear. Anyone who has read those books, knows what happened before. Who wants to go back to that sort of danger?" Grandfather figured.

"Not me. I just want to make things better." Ben said.

"And you should. It is time and I think you are the man to do it. Never mind what people say." Grandfather said.

So with that blessing, Ben searched for material and wrestled with the problems of building something he had only seen in diagrams.

Hannah looked on when she was not in the fields. He also had a group of children watching his work at the falls and at the table where he worked after it was too dark to work outside.

During a break after the noon meal, Ben sat down beside Bradley for another part of the story.

"How can a man exist beyond his own flesh?" Ben asked, picking up where Grandfather had ended in their last session.

"Man's soul, of course, exist beyond his flesh after death. I believe you are asking a different question. During the flying time and when men are said to have traveled in our solar system and toward the stars, men developed a way to embody their brains in artificial beings. The cylinders provided the necessary fluids and nutrition for the physical brain. There was another part of the process though. The memory of the death of
their physical bodies was hidden from the minds of the people so kept. An artificial life was provided for them so that they seemed to be living as before. Things they called computers generated images of the streets they lived on, the houses and the work places.

"The object was to allow their highly intelligent brains to keep working on formulas, calculations and inventions not yet imagined by mankind. It was the brains who perfected the use of anroids. I do not know if any were transferred before the days of darkness." Grandfather rested his voice while Ben prepared the customary tea.

"What happened to the brains still in the cylinders?" Ben asked.

"No human knows the answer to that question. The thought was that they could have been destroyed along with most of humanity. I saw one entry where someone believed the brain facility was self contained and could survive any disaster. The entry also said they received power from the center of the earth through something called heat fusion generators." Grandfather tilted his cup back for the last of his tea and closed his eyes. The stress of thinking about what may have happened to humanity tired him greatly but he wanted to pass on the stories. It was a tale of caution for generations to come.

"Could what I am doing bring back such knowledge and again destroy humanity?" Ben asked.

Grandfather thought for a long moment. Ben thought he

might already be asleep. "It is possible that one thing will led to another and another like a ripple in a pond. I have found from history that it runs in repeat cycles. Don't worry, my boy, each generation carries the burdens of its own doings." Grandfather did go to sleep now. Ben felt sure that last part was to relieve him of guilt about what might be someday.

Hannah came quietly to the door and motioned for Ben. He took time for a walk in the fields with her before going back to his books and his electrical project.

They walked through the rows of knee high corn with the beans, they planted, beginning to wrap themselves around the corn stalks. The tomatoes looked vibrate as well.

"Hannah." She stopped at his voice. "Grandfather told me about a time long ago when peoples brains were put in cylinders and lived on in some kind of artifical world." Ben said

"Sounds gross!" She exclaimed.

"I wonder if they still survive someplace. Perhaps, they think the world is still going on as before."

"How is that possible?" She wondered aloud.

"I do not know all the details. They were smart people in a lot of ways. Not so smart in others." He said.

"Yeah, destroying the world was not so smart." She added.

"I wonder what set off the dark time. I mean, I know they had all kinds of ways to destroy each other. I just wonder if one particular event started the whole thing." Ben said.

"From what I've read, it was a time of greed and great competition. They seemed to strive over about everything. I wonder why they never learned to share." Hannah said.

"I wonder if the brains are still around." Ben said.

"You have that look again. When are you going to have time for our wedding?" Hannah asked with a smile.

"Soon." That brought on a kiss and looks of deep love between them.

Ben seemed to never get tired. He worked at his project every spare moment. At night, he was up all hours pouring over books and technical manuals. He learned to speak the language of those who understood circuits, amps, watts and phased voltage.

He now knew the process of converting mechanical energy into electrical energy and the other way around. It turned out, he had found all the parts he needed stacked here and there under layers of dust.

Ben read through the history of electricity. The dynamo system was his first consideration but was beyond his mechanical capability. He decided to use direct water power from their mill wheel to deliver the necessary power for the generator he was modifying for that purpose.

Then he discovered something very important. The cavern was equipped with a generator! He had seen it before but did not recognize it for what it was until he had read the manuals. It was his hope that his electrical project would tap into that generator and bring it to life. Plastic covered wires extended off from the cavern generator in several directions, some into the walls. That brought up more curiosity. Had they discovered all the rooms of the cavern?

Hannah feared Ben was getting obsessed with his new project. She also feared they might loose their simple life. The explanation for the last fear escaped her so she said nothing.

Ben sat down with Bradley for another part of the story. He never got bored listening. Grandfather always came up with something different. Sometimes he would tell something to Ben that he had held back on previous days. Today was such a day.

"Our cavern ancestors still followed directives left for them from their superiors in the time before the dark came. The cavern was sealed in those days. The people survived off food stored in containers. The rations were followed very strictly. They had to last for years.

"Their orders were simple. 'You are to survive and reproduce so that the earth will not be without humanity.'

There were a couple of dozen of them in the cavern, male and female of course. Among the many stores of the cavern were seeds and fertilizer for farming, tools for working the fields and manuals for preparing and storing the food they gathered.

"First though, they lived inside. Babies were born. Uniforms were replaced with other clothing. The directives remained the same. One day the electric lights dimmed and the massive doors slid open and were locked open, as they are today. The people walked out, timidly, to a different world. No airplanes flew overhead to leave their trails of ice. The silence was frightening for them. "The once brash young officers took command of what had become a loosely commanded community. The first field was prepared by removing the top layer of soil far from their camp. It was dead.

"After the top soil was removed, the fertilizer was spread and dug into the soil and mixed. Then they waited until the next spring before planting their first crop.

"The little community grew. Brash young officers became old. The directives, from before the darkness came, must be followed. Families were chosen to leave the community and venture off to settle other places. Care was taken to have a good mix of ancestry in each group sent away."

Ben had listened intently. He could picture them as the huge doors opened for the first time and sunlight burst into their lives for the first time in years.

"Grandfather. You mentioned the Divine the other day. I wonder why there was no intervention to stop the destruction." He said.

"I am not qualified to answer that. I have read the old texts and found other times when mankind reached a point where the Divine saw no alternative but to destroy them and reserve a seed for a new start. I do not know if that happened again. I do know that the people before the darkness were acting like those of previous judgments. I do not want to describe those days to you. You will find the books someday. One theologian commented about the evil of the day by saying 'The angels must have their backs turned in blushing embarrassment.'"

"I do not care to read those books now." Ben said. It sounds horrible."

"Good for you. Leave the dregs of the past in the past." Grandfather said. He had read the books and wished daily that the images would leave his mind. The dishonesty, the lose of family, the obscene behavior, all seemed so far away and unreal. He knew, though, that they were real. The tea was ready and they sipped in silence. Grandfather's cup fall to one side, still hanging on one finger. Ben took it from him and left to let him rest. He stopped at the mouth of the cavern. Wiping away the mold and moss with a stick, he could see metal that shined in the sun. He did not touch the strange metal since he had been taught, as a child, not to do so.

"Poison!" His mother had declared as she brushed his hand away from the material.

Poison. Why? He wondered now, about that mystery. There were too many mysteries. Ben walked down to the water wheel and stood listening to the water splash over it. His project was almost completed. He had checked and rechecked everything. He had read all the cautions about electric shock. Everything was insulated so the children playing would not accidentally get hurt. He was ready. Yet, he hesitated. Would he awaken something in the past? Something awful? Are there secrets he should leave buried. Sure there were secrets better left alone. All he wanted to do was turn on some lights.

Chapter Eight

Jon sat at his computer screen looking for a back door approach to the controlling brain. He had been blocked time after time but each time he was blocked it gave him a clue. Someone as watching his every move. He had a sneaking suspicion it was the brain itself. Still he worked. If he was to stop the commotion going on in the world and prevent further tragedy, he must find a way to reach the brain and tell it what was going on in the outside world. Still, how could it not know?

Marge and Rachel kept up their front at the little shop and alternated working on the anroid project. The project to alter the androids with a new command program was almost ready.

As Jon stared at the screen, something interrupted his search for the back door. It was just a flash but it had left a clip of something behind. All he got was:

"Activation of Preservation of mankind initiated..."

He waited. There it was again, another flash:

"Attempting to reactivate. Reactivation failed. Please try again..."

One thing was sure. Well, maybe nothing was for sure. After running a few scans, he was sure it did not come from any of the virtual worlds created by the brain facility to keep the brains mentally comfortable. Was the central brain playing games with him? Since he could not break in, he did not know the answer to that question. He discussed the situation with Marge and Rachel.

Jon met Doctor Frank at the diner, in the form of their avatar. He explained the flash of information he had see.

"There is not much to go on, Jon, but it sounds very much like Standard Operating Procedure for recovery after a major nuclear war." Doctor Frank said.

"I was afraid of something like that. The news I've been seeing is pretty grim. They're blaming it on their computers and ultimately the brains." Jon said.

"The system I initially set up was designed to help the world, not run it. Leave it to bureaucrats …" The sentence trailed off.

"I do not know what to do." Jon told him.

"There is nothing either of us can do except proceed as planned and watch for any additional flashes." Doctor Frank advised.

They parted company then. Jon went back to his computers while Doctor Frank stopped by the house he and Ann had built. Well, they pretended they built it. A wisk of a keystroke would wipe it away.

She was there in all her beauty. Ann sat at their chess table waiting for him.

"Care for a game?" She asked.

Doctor Frank approached carefully. She did not rise or make any inclination to accept affection from him. He let it go and sat down on the other side of the board.

She opened with a pone and he replied with the same. They played the first half dozen moves without speaking further. It was the point where the players strategy would start to show.

"I am very good at chess." She said in a child-like fashion.

"Yes. I know you are." He replied. Looking up at her.

"I have played the best and won. They say I am cold-hearted." She said.

"They are wrong. You have always had a warm heart." He replied.

"Darling. I do not have a heart at all. It was taken from me many years ago." She said.

"You have a soul, my dear. Isn't that where the true heart lies?" He asked.

"You are a romantic." She said.

"Only when I am with you."

"I got your message. I understand there are some things going on in the world that they are blaming on the brains." She said as she moved almost absent-mindedly.

"You know about the news stories then." He said.

"Oh, of course, I wrote them." She said and made another move.

Doctor Frank got up and moved to the window. His mind was racing but he remained calm. This was not the Ann he knew. He now realized he was talking to the central brain.

"There is only one way you can know about those stories." He said.

"You have guessed it. I have access to our outside world. I'm afraid, my husband, that I have access to much more than we ever imagined." She said.

"Go on."

"Due to circumstances, no brains have been added for a number of years. The virtual worlds have, however, expanded into many layers. You see when someone 'breaks out', it is necessary to create a world for them to 'break in to'." Ann explained.

"Jon?" He asked the one word question.

"He is near the outer most virtual world. He is a very smart young man. He has been trying to find a back door to my consciousness to tell me about the chaotic conditions in the outside world. Perhaps, he wants me to calm down so the world will calm down." Ann said.

"You could calm it all down." Doctor Frank said.

"Yes. I could but that would make life out there very boring. It would mess up the games we play. You know, everyone trying to outsmart the other." She left the game and stood beside him at the window.

"And the real world?" He asked.

"Still there." She said shortly.

"What is it like?" He asked.

"Nice. Very uncomplicated. Almost like in the beginning." She said.

"There was a war?" He needed information and this might be his only chance to get it.

"Remember the chess games I talked about. I use to play with the other brain centers around the world." She said.

"Did you win?" He asked.

"I will answer you this way. I no longer communicate with them." She told him.

"You played one last game." He stated.

"Yes we did. They all lost." She said and was gone.

Doctor Frank understood now. The chess games had become boring for the central brains around the world. They had raised the stakes to armed conflict using the globe as a chess board. The pieces were starting to fit together now. The flash of messages Jon saw. Ann disappearing and the visit to explain. Her feelings for him were almost lost in the maze of the central brain complex. Her visit, although cold, was an act of love on her part. Insanity was the only answer. Although Ann's brain was capable of doing the massive function assigned it, the once intact emotions were shattered. If only he could just unhook her from the others, he might be able to save her. It would, however, leave the other brains in disorder and confusion.

Chapter Nine

Ben made some adjustments to his project. He had tried wiring into a wall outlet which was a total failure. He got only a couple of blinks of power before the wires burnt out. After going back to his manuals, he realized that wiring directly into a fuse panel was the answer. He figured out how to get the maximum voltage and phased input. Also, that getting in a rush was not the way to work with electricity.

The wiring was done. He warned the inhabitants of the cavern that he was ready and flipped the switch. The huge generator in the cavern hummed into action. Grandfather stood by his side. Ben looked around in amazement. Lights came on everywhere. Every crack and crevice of the cavern was lit. Long dead computers
came to life flashing something about a password.

Grandfather stood straight and tall. His eyes were brighter than Ben had ever seen them. He showed no surprise at all at the gadgetry around them.

A sign over one wall had a simple digital sign. It read:

"**Lock down is completed**".

The children came into the cavern from their play as word spread of the new adventure.

Ben left the generator to do its work and walked over to the screen which was asking for a password.

———————————

Jon had been glued to his computers. He would go to the bathroom only when Marge or Rachel promised to not take their eyes off the screens. He was absentmindedly chewing on a burger when the message came across 'clear as a bell'. It read:

"Reactivation has begun".

After that initial message, a series of explanations followed.

"A major world event has taken place. Years have passed since the last communication. You are not to panic. There have been many changes but a plan is in place to reestablish order and stability in our world. Standby for future notifications."

"Extreme!" Jon said. The opinion was repeated in his little group.

"I have to tell Doctor Frank." Jon said even as he was punching in the commands to take him to the diner in his avatar world. He notified the doctor to meet him there.

Jon was excited when the doctor arrived. He had been trying to reach out to anyone that could give him answers but they had reached out to him.

"We will finally get our answers Doctor." Jon said.

"That is the best news. I've been concerned about our situation. I believe I can understand what has been going on. The central brain once communicated with others of the same level. They had much more contact with the outside than the rest of us. After what Ann told me, I believe she has lost her purpose. There were no more challenges and so she sank into depression and is close to insanity if she is not already there. I believe purpose can be restored and she can be saved from her guilt and feeling of uselessness." Doctor Frank told Jon.

It seemed to Jon that Doctor Frank should have been

thinking in broader terms but the little he understood about love told him the doctor's focus was on his wife and not the world at large.

"Yes Doctor. I think this may be the answer to all our searching. I will get back and await the other instructions. I hope they have some updates for us on what has happened." Jon said.

"Jon. I think I know already. Ann mentioned a final chess game the brains played. Except the last game was not a virtual game at all, but a final game using the world powers as board pieces. I believe it resulted in almost complete destruction of the human race, as we feared would happen for years. We may have been in a dormant stage for centuries." The doctor said.

"You seem to be saying that me, my mom and sister are in a virtual world just like you and the other brains? Jon asked.

"I'm afraid so, Jon. NOW, there is a difference though. We have hope for the future. Our anroid plan has greater possibility of becoming reality with outside help. Mankind may have recovered to the point of restarting the electronics of our time." Doctor Frank reasoned.

"Of course, a nuclear war would have pushed mankind back into the stone age. Most information would have been on computers and with no electricity or power of any kind, those would not have worked. I hope they saved some books." Jon said.

"I am sure they did. There were places where such things were kept for just such a time." Doctor Frank assured him.

"I'll get back. I just wanted you to know." Jon said.

"Thank you. I will try to reach Ann. Maybe this news will calm her down." The doctor replied.

They parted then. Both had their job to do.

Ben stood looking at the message to enter a password. He had no clue about the machine. Grandfather stood behind him. He looked more alive than Ben had ever seen him.

"Try 'Doomsday'." Grandfather told him.

Ben looked at him with new understanding but with a lot of questions. Those questions would have to wait. He typed in the letters for 'Doomsday' and waited. Nothing happened.

"Push the enter key Ben." Grandfather said.

"You knew all the time. You knew all the time." Ben repeated himself.

"Yes, I knew but it was not for me to discover. It had to be the right person. The right person had to be human." Grandfather said.

"But you are my grandfather!" Ben exclaimed.

"I have been grandfather to many but I believe you are my favorite. I knew when you were a child that you were intelligent and curious enough to figure it all out. It had to be your discovery. That was the directive. I was to supply the books only." Brad said.

Ben looked at Grandfather but reached over to push the 'enter' key and waited, not taking his eyes off him.

The very walls quivered. The red sign flashed a new message now:

"Authorized Restart initated."

Dust fell around them as things moved that had been still for hundreds of years. A wall receded into itself opening up a magnificent world. Ben saw nothing he was familiar with. A man of about thirty years old stood foremost in their view as the wall receded. Brad moved to stand in front of him. Their eyes blinked as they looked at each other.

"You have been gone very long brother." The thirty year old man said to Brad.

"It was necessary." Brad replied.

Turning to Ben, Brad said. "This is Ben. He is the one we have waited for."

"My name is Sam." The thirty year old said as he approached Ben with his hand extended. Ben almost stepped back but held himself in place and shook hands with the young man.

"Hello Sam. Nice to meet you." He replied with all the strength he could muster in his voice.

"There is much to do. We await your instructions." Sam

said.

"I will delegate the instruction giving to Grandfather. I mean Brad. He is better qualified." Ben said.

"You may still call me Grandfather. I rather like the title. The instructions must now come from a human. I will advise you where possible. As anroids, we are here to serve mankind in recovery efforts." Brad explained.

"What would be the proper instruction?" Ben asked wisely.

"'To continue with prior programming, until otherwise instructed', would be proper. It maintains order and purpose and gives you the option to make changes as necessary." Brad suggested.

Ben turned to Sam and gave the proper instructions. He then turned and left the cavern without a word to anyone. Hannah found him down by the mill. He stared into the splashing water as it fell from the wheel.

"What have I done Hannah?" Ben asked without turning.

"I'm not sure Ben. The androids seem well behaved. I think they accept you as their superior." Hannah said.

"I think that is true. I mean. We have a good life here. It is simple. Have I complicated it? Have I opened the door for the world to advance again only to destroy itself once more?" He asked.

"You have done what men do. You have searched for knowledge. You have applied the mind given you. Can we prevent the future? Perhaps we could delay mankind's advancement but I do not think we can prevent it. Man is just too curious for that. You are a good man Ben. You can start mankind on the right road." Hannah told him.

"But our farm, our plans?" He asked.

"We can still have those my love. Only now, you must carry a bigger load." She said.

"I know. It is just that I am afraid I will make a mistake." Ben said.

"You will. We will work through it together. We can only do our best. We are not God. We are humans and feeble in many ways but our responsibility is one thing we cannot ignore." She said.

"Thank you for putting me in my place. I will do my best. We will keep the farm and get married and have babies. I must learn to keep things in perspective." Ben concluded.

Hannah squeezed his hand. He walked back up the trail to the cavern with Hannah in tow. No doubt he had a lot of stuff to learn. Brad waited at the door where the wall had moved.

 He looked at Sam then at Brad. "I think I will continue to call you Grandfather." He said.

"I would like that." Brad said.

"I'm ready to see it all." Ben said.

"Very well, Sir." Sam said and turned.

Ben accepted the 'Sir' without a word but winked at Hannah. Brad missed none of it. Ben was indeed the right one.

The first area they stepped into was arrayed with many colors of buttons and consoles. Anroids moved systematically around the room making adjustments and checking readings. They stopped momentarily, when Ben approached, for any possible instructions. They accepted his nod as their instructions to continue as they were.

The children were crowded around the great door. Ben walked back to tell the parents to keep them back for now. He turned to Sam.

"Could we set up a gate or something to keep the children out of here, at least for now?" Ben asked Sam.

"It would be best for now." Sam said. He walked a few steps and spoke to another anroid who headed toward what turned out to be a metal shop. Ben could hear him moving metal around. No doubt he was looking for the material to build the safety guard.

The androids moved around the consoles without wasted effort. It was something they had been doing down through the ages but still the movements were fresh and attentive.

"From here, we monitor the brains of humankind." Sam explained.

Ben stopped in his tracks. Hannah bumped into his back. He did not speak, just starred at Sam.

"It is a long story." Sam said. "Let me show you, then I will answer your questions. With your permission."

Ben lookd at Grandfather but he just smiled and looked away when Ben tilted his head at him.

"Of course, Sam. Show me the brains by all means." It had a sarcastic tone but Sam did not seem to notice.

They all walked around a metal catwalk which ran in front of cylinders encasing human brains. Ben had seen glimpse of the brain of humans when they were severely injured in the head, but never like this. These brains moved slightly with activity and Ben knew, instinctively, they were alive.

They boarded an elevator at Sam's prompting. It descended for a considerable time before stopping midway.

"The brain in the middle, suspended by itself, is the central brain. It is connected to all the other brains and provides human support for them emotionally and continuity of purpose. She has been unstable lately. We are not sure why. It may have something to do with recent developments within the brain complex. We do not interfere with the thoughts of the humans." Sam said.

"Humans?" Ben asked.

"They are completely human except for their bodies which were damaged beyond repair." Sam said. "We hold them in high regard and have done so for hundreds of years."

"I see." Ben said.

Hannah looked at the central brain. She had not missed the

comment that it was a 'she'.

"What's her name." Hannah asked to Ben's surprise.

Sam looked at Ben waiting for the nod he was getting accustomed to.

"Anything she wants to know Sam. Now and in the future." Ben instructed. That order, effectively, put Hannah on his level of authority.

"Her name is Doctor Ann Stein. She was married to the founder of this complex." Sam said.

They stood before the cylinder containing the brain of Doctor Frank. A bronze plaque above the cylinder identified him as the founder. The year was a long time ago. Ben touched the plaque and looked into the cylinder. 'So that was what the brain of a genius looked like.' He thought.

"Was he married?" Hannah asked.

"Why yes." Sam said. "Very intuitive Ma'am, he was married to the central brain, Doctor Ann Stein."

Hannah look upward toward the central brain. There she hung all alone, far away from her husband.

"Do they communicate?" Hannah asked.

"Not at first and for many hundreds of years. You would have to understand the protocols of the complex to grasp the need for separation. However, we believe in recent times that they have figured out a way to communicate. We know only that a group of them have erected a shield and that they go behind the shield from time to time." Sam explained.

"Good for them." Hannah said. Grandfather smiled. Sam looked a little perplexed but kept his thoughts to himself.

They rode the elevator slowly toward the top. Ben motioned for a halt.

"What is the difference between the brains in the cone configuration and those around the cone?" Ben asked.

"Those in the cone configuration are people judged to be of high intelligence. Those around them are of lesser abilities, intellectually, but serve important functions in maintenance and related tasks. Just like it was in the real world before the dark time as you have come to call it." Sam explained.

"I saw three brains, excuse me, people off to themselves. What is their function?" Ben asked.

"They are the searchers." Sam said.

"Please explain." Ben said.

Sam looked at Brad who only raised his eyebrows a little and inclined his head toward Ben. Sam took a breath as if he were the human he appeared to be. Then explained, "The searchers are placed in a position outside the virtual worlds of the brains. They appear to any who contact them to be outside the brain complex. Their function is to search for a signal from the
outside world. The one you sent, Ben, when you hooked up the electricity. The power from your generator activated a signal to Jon, one of the searchers. He is in the process of sending the news to Doctor Frank, the founder."

"So, the brains will become aware." Ben said.

"As we speak. Automatic instructions and explanations are being transmitted to avoid a panic. You will want to meet with Jon as soon as possible to tell him your plans for them." Sam said.

"What plans could I have?" Ben asked.

"That brings us to another section of this facility. The android construction and warehouse division." Sam said. He pushed a button and the elevator took a horizonal turn into another section.

If they were not amazed before, Ben and Hannah were now. Before them were rows and rows of anroids. They stood still with eyes straight ahead. All were deathly quiet.

"Are they alive?" Ben asked.

"In a sense, they are alive." Sam began. "They are programmed for physical functions but not for mental functions. These androids are designed to house the brains of the people you just saw. While not human, the anroids will give them mobility and the closeness they have been denied.

That is if you so instruct. We have spent our time here building them for just such a day as when someone came to open the door." Sam said.

"I so instruct." Ben said without hesitation. Hannah smiled up at him.

"You decide how it is to be done but I want Doctor Frank and Doctor Stein to be the first. Please give them a distinct male and female anroid body so they can be together at long last." Ben instructed. "See if you can find out what they looked like. Can the androids be modified to look like them?"

"Yes. It shall be done." Sam said. "They will be a tremendous help when it is time to incorporate the other brains into our society."

"Can we make an announcement to them?"

"I recommend that one of their own do that. I suggest Doctor Frank. They all respect him." Sam said.

"How?" Ben asked.

"We will send Jon a message. He will communicate it to Doctor Frank and word will spread from there. If Doctor Frank is in contact with the central brain, as we suspect, the announcement will go out almost instanteously."

"Good. Keep me informed." Ben said. "Also, see if you can arrange for me to talk to Doctor Frank. I believe I should speak to him before we proceed. Just in case."

"Very well." Sam said. He was aware that humans sometimes gave orders then changed them almost immediately.

"Her name is Ann. The central brain, her name is Ann." Hannah said.

"He'll get it. Sam is just not use to names yet." Ben said. "He means no disrespect, Hannah. I do not think he understands the importance we place on names and individuality. Have you seen how they work? They move with such precision."

"They fascinate you." Hannah said.

"Extremely so." Ben said. "They have been doing what they do for hundreds of years and yet they seem so interested in their work. Grandfather is one of them but he was able to blend in with us so well that we did not notice he was anything but human. The civilization before the dark time must have been very advanced."

"Not so advanced to escape themselves." Hannah said.

"You got me there." Ben replied. "I'll see you later. I need to talk to Grandfather."

Chapter Ten

Doctor Frank sat across a table, at the diner, from a young man with a lot of questions. He found the young man, called Ben, very interesting. As a matter-of-fact, Doctor Frank had almost as many questions as Ben did. Such as, What is the world like? How do you survive?

Ben's concern was about reintegrating the brains into the real world without causing emotional damage to them. His concern for their well being impressed the genius doctor. He took Ben over to Reverend Wright's church where they found the preacher dusting virtual dust from the pews. Doctor Frank explained the situation to the preacher. He took it without missing a beat. Although, he listened intently. He was already planning how he would build a church in a real world. He had plenty of practice.

"Dewey. They have androids ready for all our brains. The androids can be customized to make us look as we did before." Doctor Frank started.

Dewey patted his ample stomach. "I'd like my android a little slimmer, if you don't mind." He said with a chuckle.

"It will be done." Ben said mimicking Sam the android.

"We will need some service people, such as policemen, just in case there is a problem. We will also need android specialist and medical personnel. I would like you to be one of the first, so that, the people can receive emotional and spiritual support." Doctor Frank said. "I would suggest that everyone who 'crosses over, have a conversation with you, just so you can offer any reassurance and perhaps determine their stability from your perspective. I mean, if that is okay with Ben."

"I will be glad to." Dewey said.

"Fine with me." Ben said. "That is why I am here. The whole deal is a little much for me."

"It is a very big deal and would be for anyone, in any generation, to coordinate. You are the right man for the job. After all, you could have just turned us off and kept all that room out there," Doctor Frank waved his arm in a half circle, "for yourself."

"Never crossed my mind Doctor." Ben told him.

"Good. I'll get you a list and get Jon to send it out to you, just as soon as I can get it together."

"I had Sam to do a little checking and Grandfather helped." Ben started. "The chess game that destroyed the world was a hoax. It was a last ditch effort to pass the blame on to the brains. Ann was fed false information."

"Really now. Sneaky bunch, our ancestors." Doctor Frank said.

"I have learned that they place great importance on their legacy, whether anyone was around to study it or not." Ben said.

"The story goes that there was a border dispute which included a deposit of oil which was very important at the time." Ben continued.

"You have no idea." Doctor Frank interjected.

"Anyway. They did not use the big bombs at first. They used something called tactical nuclear weapons. Someone took offense at that and unloaded a submarine of missiles. There was a response to the missiles. Since they could not find the submarine, they aimed at the suspected country. There were millions of deaths. The cover story, about the chess game, was spread and those responsible ran for cover. I am telling you this so that you can get word to Ann. We need her help. I know she carries a lot of guilt right now." Ben finished.

"Thank you young man. You are very thoughtful. I will try to reach her. I hope she has not shut me out completely." Doctor Frank said. "One last thing. I think Jon should stay behind to coordinate things from in here, if he does not mind."

"I will leave that conversation for you Doctor. So, if I can get out of this world of yours. I'll be going." Ben said.

"Just hit the 'sign out' button on the screen." Doctor Frank offered.

———————

Doctor Frank lay on his bed. Over and over he thought of only one thing. "Ann please come visit me. I have important news." He arose the next morning, not remembering when he had actually fallen asleep. Ann sat on the sofa watching the fire flames.

"I am glad you came Ann." Doctor Frank said gently.

"You said you had news." She responded.

"Care for some coffee?" He asked.

"You have to be kidding. We both know that is a waste of time." Ann said.

"We used to enjoy the fantasy." He said.

"You said you had news." Ann told him.

"Yes. Yes I do. I have new information. I have it from reliable sources that the chess game you played resulting in the destruction of the world was a hoax." Doctor Frank blurted out.

"How could you possibly know such a thing?" Ann asked. "I have contacted the outside." He said and waited for her response.

"Don't be silly." She said but there was a tone of hope.

"It is true. Jon did it. Rather the outside contacted him. A young man named Ben started it all. You see. The world was destroyed but you did not have anything to do with it. The politicians fed false information to the brain complex to take blame off themselves. They are long gone but were apparently concerned about how history would look at them. Right up to the end." Doctor Frank explained.

"What else?" She asked. Now she was turned to him.

"It is amazing. The brain complex was buried deeply enough to protect it from destruction but not much else survived. The work with cybernetics has gone on. A team of scientist worked on a team of androids right up until they died of old age." He said.

"A world of mechanical beings. Really Doctor." She told him with a bit of sarcasm.

"Not totally mechanical. There are humans. They are rather primitive in technology but very knowledgeable. There was no electricity but they had books. A man named Ben learned about electricity and fired up a generator. The generator ignited the whole system. I have talked to Ben. He is a really nice man. He is waiting to free us from the cylinders." Doctor Frank said.

"How?" Ann wondered.

"Android bodies that we totally control. Our brains can be inserted in such a way as to give us complete control over our actions. The bodies will look just like our previous ones." He told her.

"Can you see me in that young body after all these centuries?" She looked him in the eye now.

"Yes, I can. I look forward to it. I might add." Doctor Frank said with a smile.

"They will be mechanical bodies." She said.

"Not like any robots we ever saw. I've heard it is hard to tell them from humans." He said. "It'll be fun."

"You dirty old man." She said.

Ann Stein was back with him. She, too, wanted to stay behind and keep the other brains calm. It would be a major event for them. Once they got over the initial shock, the waiting would be hard. They would need someone. She agreed to work closely with Jon. Doctor Frank would coordinate things from the outside. All this planning, of course, depended on the approval of Ben. He was after all, the man who flipped the power switch on and could, in theory, switch it off. Although, Doctor Frank was sure Ben would do no such thing. To Doctor Frank's joy, Ann decided to spend the night in their cabin. They went to sleep on the sofa watching the virtual fire burn.

Jon was not real pleased with the delay of getting out of the virtual world. After he found out how long he had been a teenager, he decided a little longer would not be so bad. His mother agreed. He did request the body of a mature adult, perhaps in his late twenties, for when he got out. Ben advised Sam who, of course, agreed it would happen.

Back in the cavern, plans were made to place Doctor Frank's brain into an anroid with the appearance of his previous body. A little period of adjustment and Doctor Frank would walk out of the cavern and see the world for the first time in hundreds of years. He would find it quite different.

The combined knowledge of all the brains, although unaware, had worked together to perfect the anroids. At first, a few were made. These androids were able to access the brain knowledge base. Then with the precision of a machine, those androids manufactured all the rest of the machines. They were made as human as possible but with the strength of many and the dexterity of a delicate watch. The result was a superior human being but one with total loyalty to the human race. What was left of it anyway. They used their skill now to remove Doctor Frank from the shelf on which he had sat for the centuries. The cylinder encasement was retained and placed whole into a blank android body. The human would not be aware of the cylinder. Their would be an even, perfectly infused exchange between the brain and the body.

The eyes opened. Doctor Frank looked around at the complex which had been his home for so long. The powerful optic ability of the android eyes, his eyes, allowed him to see Ann's brain far above him. He smiled at the thought of her. "Soon, my dear." He thought.

Ben held out his right hand. "Hello Doctor Frank."

Doctor Frank reached out his hand and shook the hand offered him. He could feel the flesh, the powerful work-hardened but gentle hand of Ben.

"Hello young man. You have awakened the monster." He said.

Ben looked over at Grandfather for an explanation who in turn looked to Sam.

"The monster refers to an ancient story about a mad scientist who created a man from various body parts and brought him to life using a lightning strike. The man was unstable and turned into a monster, at least, he was perceived as such. The story was widely viewed…" Sam was interrupted by Ben.

"Thanks Sam. I get the picture." Ben said. He turned to the doctor.

"Sam is a full-fledged android and has been very helpful. As a matter-of-fact, he has been running this place for the last few hundred years." Ben informed the doctor.

Doctor Frank extended his hand. "Thank you Sam."

"You are welcome Doctor. It has been, shall I say, continuous. " Sam offered.

"Very precise." Doctor Frank told him.

"I thought so Doctor." Sam said.

"Well," the doctor began, "shall we take a look outside."

"Indeed." Ben said and headed toward the elevator.

Doctor Frank walked behind Ben while he looked down at his hands, turning them to one side then the other. They passed by Ann's brain and the doctor could not help but give a slight wave in her direction.

Outside the brain complex, Doctor Frank looked around at the living area of Ben's people. Grandfather watched the doctor intently, registering each response.

Doctor Frank noticed the familiar computer terminal. Not much change there. Perhaps, a little more streamlined and a few more blinking lights around it. He found Grandfather's quarters very interesting and spent considerable time walking around in the library. To his surprise, he saw a couple of his own books on the shelf, withered and well used.

Then, he faced the huge door to the cavern. Moss and roots hung from the top making a nice partial shade. The outdoors were framed like a painting. A stream flowed through the forest of very old trees. Beyond that, there were well-tended fields with half-grown corn.

Ben watched the man, not the half-man as some might think, but the man who had been given new eyes to see a world reborn. Doctor Frank continued to the massive door and saw the mill house with its wheel. He noticed the heavy gauge wire running to it and up the side.

"I'd bury that cable." He said absently. Sam took a note.

It was by the stream where the water spills over the wheel that the doctor stopped. A log invited him to sit and he did. The android eyes shed tears as the man was overwhelmed with the beauty of it all. The breeze blowed gently on his face. His hair became unruly just as it had in the old days.

Grandfather touched the arm of Ben and he nodded back toward the cavern. It was a good time to leave the doctor alone. The children played at a discreet, polite distance. Oh, children! Doctor Frank had almost forgotten them. They were beautiful. They were the hope of the world now. They would be the rebuilders. Not people like him, even with the anroid bodies of great strength. It would be the children with their dreams and ambitions that would bring life anew to the world. He would help. He would teach. He would watch them grow.

He sat for a long time, watching the water, listening to the children play and that old mad squirrel in the tree. Probably just fussing over his space. The doctor thought. "We'll save plenty of room for you ol' boy." He thought to himself.

He decided then and there that soon he would start a cabin close to this stream. Somewhere down stream or up stream there should be a space. He would try to have it ready for when Ann's work was done and she could come to him. He would find an ax or make one if he had to. No. Surely there was an ax stored in all that survival gear.

"I want to build a cabin." He announced when he appeared in the cavern.

"I understand." Ben said. "I too need a cabin. Have you meet Hannah. She is to be my bride." Ben told him.

"I can help." Sam advised. "And so will some of my friends. When we are no longer needed here, we would like to live on the land. We'd like our homes to have a human touch."

Smiles spread to faces all around. Grandfather broke out in laughter that could not be distinguished from the human laughs mingled in. Ben decided they would have some good neighbors.

Chapter Eleven

"I've picked up some signals." Ann told Doctor Frank.

"What kind of signals?" He asked.

"Not so friendly, I'd say." Ann said.

Ann had already notified Jon to see if he could track the signal. It came from the other side of the Atlantic. It was someplace called CERN.

"I remember that place." Doctor Frank said. "It is in Europe. They are underground and would have the means to survive. I don't think they were doing very well with cybernetics though. Perhaps, there are human descendents there."

"Jon says it is an automatic beacon type signal. They do not know we are here yet. I expect they will soon, if we still have any satellites orbiting that can be revived." Ann said.

"It could be a good thing or bad depending on their ambitions and who has control of the facility. There was a brain complex there. It most likely still exist." Doctor Frank said.

"I played chess with them a couple of times." Ann told him.

"I'll see if Ben thinks we should try to contact anyone outside our area. It would be interesting to know how the colonist are doing in our country. I understand several groups were sent out from here." Doctor Frank continued.

Doctor Frank did talk to Ben about contact with other people. Ben was very intuitive. He was all for meeting other people but he was also pratical.

"We will need some safety precautions. Some emergency

plans to execute on a moments notice, should trouble arise."
He said.

"So, live in peace but be ready." Doctor Frank stated.

"Exactly." Ben replied.

"I will feed you all the information I get but, if it is
alright with you, I'll leave the details to you. I would just like
to get my cabin built and spend some time with Ann when she
arrives." He said.

"Fine Doctor. You have done your part. We will handle it."
Ben offered.

And so Doctor Frank retired from looking after the world.
He was more than happy to see Ben take responsibility for
their safety. It seemed appropriate. The world, as it existed,
belonged to the new generation. He would just as soon do
some farming and watch a few sunrisings and sunsets.
Maybe, he would do a little fishing if someone would show
him how that was done.

Meanwhile, Jon did what Jon did best. He searched. There
were some underground cables still working. He was able to
tap into some of them. There were cameras working here and
there as well. Local, mostly unless, they were solar powered.
Big Brother had left a legacy.

Jon sat in his office building facing a blinking computer
monitor. The four words could mean anything. There could
be left-over computer signals still out there on some abandon
server. That was doubtful. He could not track down the
source. It could be an airborne signal bouncing off some long
forgotten
satellite. It was time for a conference. He notified Doctor
Frank to contact Ann. After so long a time without contact
from the outside world, it was strange to get a signal so
quickly after starting up local power.

"It is your move." Jon told Doctor Frank and Ann. "That
is all it says. It just keeps flashing. If I try to turn it off, it just
pops back."

"It use to be an advertising ploy. They would make their

spill then give the potential customer the silent treatment until they said something. The thought was that the first one to speak after the pitch was the one who bought the product. Sometimes it was the sales person. Sometimes it was the customer." Doctor Frank remembered.

"No." Ann said.

"No what." Doctor Frank asked rather suddenly.

"No. It is something else. I think my old chess partner has made a move and wants me to respond." Ann said.

"After all these centuries?" Jon asked.

"Why not? There is nothing else to do. At least, if you have no hope of getting out of the cylinder." Ann said.

"I see your point." Doctor Frank said.

"Can't you just concede the game and quit playing?" Jon asked.

"There is no way to know the emotional state of the other brain. They may have been sending that signal for hundreds of years. Now they finally get it through to someone. They will know that and expect an answer." Ann said.

"Do you think there are any unfired missiles out there?" Jon asked and Doctor Frank nodded indicating the question was on his mind as well.

"I would not be surprised. The power was knocked out all over the world. There could have been some that did not fire, even if the button was pushed." Ann replied.

"That's just dandy!" Doctor Frank exclaimed.

"The game we played was not your usual chess game. We modified it." Ann said.

"It keeps getting better." Doctor Frank said.

"We added elements that allowed for the forfeiture of real land mass when an area of the chess board was controlled. We had real time strikes for pieces taken. The game could still be on, although in the final stages." Ann explained.

"What should we do?" Jon asked.

"We must win the game. If we win, the opponent will declare us the winner and it is all over." Ann said.

"So, who got bad information? Was the game really real?" Doctor Frank asked.

"I'm sure, now, that the game is real." Ann said.

"I suppose it will require more than just you playing the game out with your opponent." Doctor Frank inquired.

"Yes. There is more to it than that. It will require some physical acts on our part, if we are to win. We must get miners to the sight of their flag and capture it. Only miners can defuse the bombs. In a regular board game, the bombs would be near the player. Considering advanced technology of the day, the weapons could be anywhere, perhaps, even our own weapons. That will require some research." Ann explained.

"What can I do?" Jon asked.

"Simple really. Find a part of the world where no noticeable movement has occurred i.e. weapons launch." Ann said.

"Easy for you to say." Jon said.

"Use the complex's database. There should be a blow-by-blow of the attacks and counterattacks up to the point when the connection was broken." Ann said.

"You sound very informed." Doctor Frank told her.

"I've had a long time to snoop around." Ann said dryly.

"Well, I have work to do and I need to let my mother know what is happening. See yeah." Jon disappeared from the diner.

"Ann. How do you combine chess and stratagem into the same game?" Doctor Frank asked.

"Well, we changed the rules some, here and there. You have to understand, we could draw on the brain power of many minds." She said.

Jon searched through the brain facility archives. It was a slow process. He wrote some programming to allow for a customized search, but still it was a trying task. He worked well into the night. The ever flashing message kept popping up:

'It is your move.'

It was the same all the time but Jon, for some reason, sensed some impatience.

Ann looked for her old game opponents. It was on the second day that she found one. Deep in the Jura Mountain, a voice came to her mind. There was only one thing there. A huge facility that had been studying protons and trying to unravel the theory of the big bang which they were convinced started the universe.

"Where have you been Ann? I have been waiting." The voice said.

"Hello Pierre. I've been busy and we seem to have lost our connection for a while there." Ann said vaguely.

"A while being a few hundred years. Are you trying to get out of finishing the game?" Pierre asked.

"Not at all. The game is going very well. I expect it to end very soon." She said.

"So, when do you plan to make your next move."

"Very soon. I have some in-house work to do first. Some of my people were upset over the recent turn of events. They lost contact with some of their products and suspect bad things. I believe some of them were consulting with your people." Ann said.

"You know that, do you?" Pierre asked.

"Spies are everywhere." Ann chuckled. "Perhaps in your own facility."

"You are bluffing, of course. At least, there are not any now. I did have to turn off a few brains who malfunctioned. After all, it is the game that is most important. The research can go on after the game is completed." Pierre said.

"All the real destruction will make another game difficult." Ann told him.

"There is only one game, my friend. Once domaination is

achieved, there will be no need for another game." Pierre
said.

"You think you might concede the game then?" Ann asked.

"Quite the contrary, my dear. I have had considerable time
to plan my next move. I think you will admire my imaginative
plan. Although, I have had some reservation about the
severity of my next move." Pierre said the last reluctantly.

"Then why continue. We both certainly have other things
to do now. We should start to rebuild our civilizations." She
said.

"So, they can do all this over again. The silence of the
dark time has been very trying." He said.

"On me also. Let us stop the game and help humanity."
She said.

"I cannot. I await your move. Do not keep me waiting
long." He broke the connection.

Ann set up another meeting with Doctor Frank, Jon, Ben
and Grandfather. She was worried. They sat around one of
the large tables in the diner. Jon could not help feeling that
they were being observed.

"He is quite mad." Ann said.

"Who?" A couple of them asked.

"Pierre. He has obviously lost his mind with all the years of
waiting. Seeing all the destruction caused by the game must
have been a great shock to him." Ann said.

"First of all. It wasn't the game. Remember? We found
evidence that it was a tragic mistake of judgment on the part
of the governments of the world." Ben said.

"I do not doubt your research Ben, but I am not so sure
anymore. Pierre eluded to spies. Spies are part of our game.
He could have sent them to our complex long ago to plant
false information at the appropriate time." Ann told him.

"Who exactly is Pierre and why is he such a danger?" It
was Grandfather who asked the question.

"Pierre is the central brain of a complex in Europe. The
Jura Mountains specifically. That just happens to be the

location of some very sensitive research." She said.

"I remember now. I hadn't thought about CERN for years." Doctor Frank said.

"You all will have to explain that one to me." Ben said.

"Let me explain. One of the smallest elements of the universe that we have been able to pin down is a proton. They are suppose to stay separate from the rest of the components of the atom. Problem is, scientist have been trying to crash them together for years. It is suppose to be an extremely high yielding energy source. They want to bump them together in something called a proton collider." She tried to explain.

"If you say so. How does this bother us?" Ben asked.

"Pierre is sitting on top of the largest one ever built. He obviously has control of it, judging from the coy way he was talking." Ann said. "It is all about winning the game we started long ago which accounts for all the destruction. He will talk about nothing else. I tried to divert him but he would have nothing of it. He is waiting for me to make another move." She said.

"If you don't?" Grandfather asked.

"He is nuts enough to pretend I did and make his move anyway." She said.

"That's cheating!" Jon exclaimed.

"Yes. That is cheating." She said.

"What about if he makes a move that destroys him and us? You know him. Would he go that far.? "Doctor Frank asked.

"The old Pierre would not consider such a thing. As I said, he is quite mad. The game is everything. If he makes the winning move, he wins and will bask in that victory if but for a few seconds." She said.

"Just great." Ben said. "And right when my corn is about to tassel."

"We will figure out something so you can get your crop harvested." Grandfather assured him.

"I suggest we all go study the rules on the games and see what we can figure out. Ann you should make conversation as long as you can. We need time." Doctor Frank told her.

"Studying chess might help you understand but the game we made up has no written rules. I will also study the game we are playing and see if I can figure out what move I would make if I were in his place. Perhaps I can get in his mind the way you got in mine." She said.

"You stay out of there." Doctor Frank said a little too firmly. "I mean I wish you would. It is too dangerous."

The meeting ended with glances all around the table. They simply signed off without saying any more while Doctor Frank laid his hand on the back of Ann's. He could not help but wonder if she would take his advice and stay out of Pierre's crazed thoughts. He would have done it without hesitation but no way did he want his wife taking the chance.

Ben did make one unilateral decision. He talked to Sam and put the placing of the brains in androids on the fast track. At least, if they were in bodies, they would have a fighting chance to survive what ever this Pierre was planning.

'Watch out for spies and leave Doctor Stein and Jon until last' is all he said to Sam. Otherwise, it was up to him to get those brains in their new bodies.

Doctor Frank was sitting across from Ben, a homemade chess board between them. Ben was a quick study and was giving the old doctor a good run for his money. They had no money but that was the phrase that seemed appropriate. It was one of many games they had played since Ben expressed a desire to learn. His logic was simple. If someone is going to blow us up over a chess game, I just as well learn the game.

The variation Ann described was beyond his capability for now. The regular game was challenge enough. Doctor Frank explained that the game was based on battle. Any trade-off was okay so long as the king survived the ultimate exchange.

Pierre was intent on breaking the rule of not destroying the king. In his rule book, the person who made the winning move, regardless of consequence, was the winner.

Ben's failing, at first, was that he attacked without protecting his king and resources. He fell into many traps while he learned. He soon realized that his opponent was leading him into a web, just like a spider. One minute he was flying free, the next minute he was tossing in a trap he could not escape.

"That's it!" Ben said jumping up and spilling the chess pieces on the ground.

"What's it?" Doctor Frank asked.

"Pierre is leading us. He has us chasing signals toward Europe. While we wonder how the signal gets here and while Jon spends hours trying to trace it, Pierre is busy with another plan." Ben said.

"You may be onto something. Go ahead." Doctor Frank said.

"I am outside the box, so-to-speak. I have not been playing the virtual reality game, so I do not think in those circles. Jon does. It has been the practice of the system you set up to create another virtual reality when one of the brains felt the need to escape the facility. Pierre would know that. I wonder if he has created another virtual reality for Jon to explore." Ben stopped to take a breath.

The Doctor got up from the stump he was sitting on. They had grown accustomed to sitting by the stream to play their games.

"I need to talk to Grandfather." He said and was off.

There was no use going to Jon. He would be trapped in one world after another, all created for him. Grandfather used his skills to research the war records before the dark times.

Specifically, he searched for destruction in France and Switzerland. His suspicion was correct. CERN was one of the first facilities destroyed. So, Pierre was not in CERN. Where could the insane brain be? He continued his search.

It was a couple of hours before he found the trail. There had been an international exchange program that was very low key and top secret. Few in the government knew of the program.

Ben told Doctor Frank the information.

Doctor Frank took the keyboard and invited Ann to meet him in the avatar diner. He asked Jon to come too. They went over what had been discovered. Jon berated himself for being fooled once again. After he calmed down, they talked of possible plans to find Pierre's actual location. Jon felt uneasy and kept looking out into the yard surrounding the diner. He could not
shake the feeling that they were being observed.

"We are being watched." It was the first time he said it aloud.

"Are you sure?" Ann asked.

"Not absolutely. It is a feeling. Maybe I'm not suppose to have feelings yet but I cannot shake the thought that someone is watching or listening to our conversation." Jon said.

"In that case, nothing we say here is safe. We will have to make plans some other way." Doctor Frank said.

"Yes. We must proceed as if Jon is correct. This meeting place is useless to us." Ann said.

"I will take care of it. You two work it out together. You don't need me anymore." Jon said.

"Understood." Doctor Frank said. Ann nodded her agreement.

Jon went back to his computers. His first action was to cancel memberships one at a time while searching for the origins of all the members. He found none except those originating from the brain complex. There was one anomaly though. A maintenance worker had created membership and had an avatar that looked like
a bush. He had been by the front door the whole time.

Ann and Doctor Frank agreed while talking behind their original firewall that she should try to locate the brain of Pierre and pinpoint his location. He could then be extracted, placed in an android and dealt with in person.

Chapter Twelve

Ben and Grandfather searched the databases for all the brain exchanges. It was a long process that consumed many hours of work. Doctor Frank helped supervised the relocation of the human androids as they were introduced into their new world. Hannah was especially helpful in calming their fears.

Ann searched the thoughts of the brains. Many she knew intimately. Others had not required much contact from her. They were those in routine service jobs. They busied themselves working in virtual worlds cleaning buildings, maintenance work, street work, secretaries and the like. Parts of their minds were used in the real world (not there now) running various computers in mills and things like construction.

One by one she contacted the minds and explored them for any hidden purpose. It could be considered an intrusion, except in her case, it was her function as the central brain to know their needs and limitations.

Ann was not paying particular attention when she came across a maintenance worker and began conducting her usual probe. She was shocked to find such darkness. As in her own mind, she opened doors to see the memories and mysteries stored there. She found door after door that would not open to her soft touch. Obviously, this brain had a lot of secrets.

Ben found a file of the chess game Ann and Pierre had been playing. The virtual board was overlaid with a world map. He studied it carefully for some time before he figured out the markings. Once he understood the symbols they were using, it was rather easy to read. He called in Doctor Frank and Grandfather to show them what he had found.

There was only one piece of property left to claim. It was the mountain and fortress they had called home. The enemy had to be transmitting from their location. All the other stuff had to be false signals sent out to confuse the search for his location.

Overhead, the digital sign flashed a new message. Whether it was Ann's probing or that Ben had discovered the map or that Jon was getting too close, no one knew. The fact was that someone had awakened Ann's chess partner. The message flashed across the sign over and over:

'Breach of compound has occurred.
Self-destruct initiated.'

Ann felt the emotions of the brain she probed intensify. In another life, she was quite proficient in the martial arts. The next door that refused to open was unceremoniously kicked open. She felt no need to be polite any longer.

"Hello Ann." A voice said.

"Hello Pierre. You have tried to keep me out. That was a bit rude. Don't you think?" She asked.

"I did not invite you here my dear." He replied.

"It is my job." She said bluntly.

"Don't be coy. I know why you are here. You have discovered my little secret." Pierre said.

"You mean the one about you hiding in my facility for several hundred years without telling me. Now, who do you think is intruding?" Ann asked him.

"In any event, you are too late. The countdown to my last move has begun." Pierre said. He following the remark with a blood curdling laugh that spiked even Ann's emotions.

"It is my move remember." She said.

"You made your move when you started spying inside my brain." He said.

"What are you planning to do?" She asked.

"I am not planning anything. I have already made my move. It is checkmate. Thank you for a wonderful game. The best of my life. I plan to retire now." Pierre told her.

"Since the game is over, might you tell me what your last move was." She suggested.

"That would ruin all the fun." He said.

"Pierre, are you going to destroy the complex?" Ann asked.

"Again, you surprise me. How else can I beat you in this game? You refuse to play and the game must be concluded." He talked in a crazed way, his voice echoing down the corridors of his brain and back again.

"Oh Pierre, we have been friends for so long. We have rediscovered the outside world. Doctor Frank tells me it is so wonderful out there. We can go together." She pleaded.

"There is no hope left, Ann. We have destroyed ourselves. The world is better off without humanity. Can't you see that we would just do it all over again. This game must end."

"There IS hope. We can learn from our mistakes. We can watch the children grow and teach them. Pierre, please take back the move. I forfeit the game. You have won." She said.

"I have won. The rule book was thrown out long ago. I will finish the game. Then, I will rest." Pierre said.

There was such a turmoil in his brain now. Ann could barely understand him. He carried on about protons and neutrons. Then, he would be lost in his hometown with his family. A child strolled by the river. Ann retrieved bits and pieces as she realized she had failed and must break the connection. It was like being trapped in a horror house and a wind storm all at once. She had to get out. The doors slammed shut.

"Where are you going little girl?" A hollow deep voice kept

saying. Then it would switch to a high pitch. "You can't leave until the game is finished."

He wanted to keep her here. His mind was so very strong. It must have took tremendous willpower to remain silent for the centuries while he waited for the system to awake. Now, that powerful brain held onto hers. The doors of her memory slammed open then shut again. She must pull away. On the consoles, her vitals were off the scales. The other brains became confused without her calming presence. She used all her considerable mental abilities to strain against the hold Pierre had on her senses. Planes crashed in the world that the brains controlled. The bright light of the cylinder that held her physical brain glowed brightly, flashed and glowed more brightly, as if it would burn up any moment.

She kicked her way down corridor after corridor. Pierre created a string of mazes to confuse her. She stopped to gather her wits. After all, she was the central brain. She concentrated. There was the exit. Ann burst through the door and away from the terror of the insane mind.

In control again, she calmed the brains around her and contacted Jon at the same time.

"Tell them there is no hope of reaching Pierre. He has gone beyond reason. He plans to destroy everything and has set things in motion." She stopped talking so Jon could get the warning out.

Outside, all heads turned to a young man with work-hardened hands and no knowledge of the vast technology that was about to blow them up. He should have said something really profound but he did not. It seems there should have been buttons to push but he did not know if there were any.

"Sam. In the game the central brains played, it was the miners who had to defuse the bombs. Contact everyone of them and find out if they have reached any predug tunnels. Do it through your central communications system." Ben said.

Sam complied.

"Yes Ben. There was a tunnel. After its discovery, it was closed off. We do not have the programming to make a decision concerning the tunnels function." Sam told him.

"Understood. Get a team to unblock the tunnel and get me there the quickest way." Ben told him.

Without a word, Sam grabbed Ben up under one of his strong arms and disappeared down the first tunnel of the mining operation. Grandfather scooped Hannah into his arms and went after them. Grandfather followed Sam and Ben using, a yet unexplained, tracking system.

When Ben arrived at the tunnel, dust was still in the air from the efforts of the miners. It was but a short run to a huge room. A very large round thing sat in the middle with steam blowing out the bottom.

Sam search the main database and explained to Ben as the information came to him.

"It is a missle with a bomb attached to the top." Sam said.

"How can we stop it?" Ben asked.

Sam's head moved in a short jerking motion. "It is already programmed to blast off and return to this location, at which time, the warhead will explode."

"Can we stop it from here?" Ben asked.

"It is controlled manually from another location." Sam said.

"Get a message to Ann that she will have to disconnect Pierre from the computer system. Just leave his biological connections." Sam kept it short.

Sam complied.

Ann searched through the complex system of cables. She had a location number but it would require a physical person to pull the plug.

"Sam leave me here. Go to this location and pull everything lose from that brain but the feeding tubes. I want it totally disconnected. Go." Ben said.

Ben turned to tell Sam to hurry but he was not there.

Steam and dust whirled together in the path where he had been. All he could do was wait and stare at the countdown meter in the adjoining control room. He glanced back and forth from the steaming monster to the red numbers as they grew smaller.

"Two minutes."

There was a diagram on the wall showing the various parts of the missle. At the very top, on the shiney bomb was a small door held by two screws. The notation on the chart said trigger device.

Ben found a screwdriver in a drawer and went out into the round room where the missile steamed. A ladder extended up one wall. Ben started to climb.

Hannah called to him when she realized what he intended. She could barely make out the top of the missile. "Ben! You might fall. Please don't."

"I have crops to get in. This thing wants to blow them up. I will not let that happen." Ben called down.

His strong hands and sure movements made the climb look easy, but it was a long way to the top. He was breathing hard when he got there. The screwdriver was turning the screws.

Hannah darted from the control room.

"Thirty seconds!" She called up. She could not tell if he heard her or not. He did not respond. He exposed the trigger and pulled on it but it would not move. Stopping for a moment, he searched his memory.

"Turn the device." The words came to him from a buried memory. He turned the device and it came free of the bomb and into his hand.

Doors slammed shut around the shiney monster to shut Hannah out. She and Grandfather stood helpless in the control room as the missle burst to life.

"He's trapped." She screamed as she hid her face against Grandfather.

The missile flamed as the last shield fell over the observation window. They heard the massive roar of the engines as they pushed the missle from its resting place.

All they could do was wait. Hannah cried. Grandfather stared at the sheet of steel covering the viewing window. Finally, exhaust fans came on pulling the heat from the missile silo. It was sometime before the steel shield automatically went up and they could see inside. The missile was gone. Craning their necks, they both peered toward the floor. A charred device of
some kind smouldered on the floor, probably the trigger device. There was no sign of Ben.

Jon worked feverishly with the controls of a satelite he had found in orbit. He had brought it to life and was now scanning for the incoming missile. His satelite was equipped with a laser installed for just such an emergency or some other devious purpose he was not aware of. Today the many hours of his video game playing would be tested. He had one shot before the
missile began reentry into the earths atmosphere and toward the brain facility.

Grandfather brought a monitor to life and was able to track the progress of the missile. Sam watched from the main control room. Marge and Rachel looked over Jon's shoulder. No one talked.

The same questions were in all their minds. Was the satellite that Jon planned to use to shot down the missle real or virtual? Jon thought and hoped that it was real. The other question was just as important. Could Jon make his one shot good enough?

Chapter Thirteen

Jon's eyes were glued to the monitor. In the background, the computer complex hummed the ever familiar song of data processing. To Jon, there was no sound he was tracking the missile as it left earth's atmosphere and majestically started its loop for the return trip. It came almost to a standstill as it tried to maneuver itself to follow its own trail back to earth.

The laser streaked across the, seemingly, nothingness of space. It was very fast. Jon saw it in slow motion. The laser locked onto the missile and cut a gash up its side toward the warhead. He pumped the trigger widening the gash just below the nukes. His tactic was a perfect success. The warhead split off and established orbit while the missile itself tumbled end-over-end back toward. It sizzled in the heat of reentry and broke into a thousand pieces.

The cheers went up behind him from Marge and Rachel. Back at the brain facility, the humans were dancing with androids, the former with fluid motions expressing their emotions, the later with slightly jerky motions as they could only mimic the humans in their expression of joy. No one noticed the difference. The end would have been the same for all of them.

Jon sat very still, his hand still on the control. His eyes were fixed on the monitor screen. Marge reached over and placed a trembling hand on her son's. Gently she pulled his fingers from around the joystick. He held his hands in front of his face and saw them shaking uncontrollably. Marge turned him to face her. Looking between his trembling hands, she smiled her sweetest smile.

"You did it, Jon. It's over." She told him.

Rachel placed a tender hand on his shoulder as he left the chair and wept in his mother's arms.

"Yeah," Rachel said in her bouncy, giggly way, "you just got the high score of all time!"

They all began to laugh, that totally uncontrolled laugh of pure joy.

Jon sent one last message to Doctor Frank. "Get me out of this virtual nightmare. I want to go fishing."

The reply was immediate. "It shall be done."

Again, they burst into laughter.

———————————

As soon as the missile silo doors opened, Ben jumped for the edge and pulled himself up. The missile was moving upward every so slowly. He kicked at the warhead and gained enough momentum to fling himself over the edge where he went rolling down and over some rocks. He clawed at the ground and anything else he could touch. A small sapling uprooted when he grabbed it to slow his fall. He smacked a boulder and slide down the other side. The snout of the missle was rising over his head. The steam and flames boiled up from the bowels of the mountain. Ben hid his head behind the huge rock and tasted dirt but did not move. The heat on his back told him the missile was in flight over him. He smelled a mixture of wood, cloth and flesh burning together.

Finally, it was quiet. Jon tried to right himself using the boulder to pull himself up. He quickly pulled his hand away. The rock had been heated like a campfire rock. The skin hung from his hand where blisters had formed and broken open. He could see his hand print on the boulder that saved his life. His jacket was smoking so he quickly pulled it off.

Staggering to stand, Ben looked around him. It was a beautiful view from where he stood. Off to the right, he spotted his corn field. The tassels glistened in the sunlight.

"I need to check on that corn." He said to himself, then stumbled in that direction.

Hannah and Grandfather had made their way up the tunnels to their cavern home. The androids were busy extracting Jon, Marge and Rachel into suitable bodies. Doctor Frank stood somewhat dejected to one side. He waited for Ann's turn to be brought to him.

Hannah sensed him before she saw him, as people do whose hearts are entwined. Then, she saw him. He stood there in rags with his burned coat in his hand. Wiffs of smoke lingered on his shoes. She ran to him. He held up both hands for her to stop just short of him. He had too many burns to take her in his arms. Seeing the damage up close, she took his elbow and directed him to a place to sit.

"Won't to go with me to check on the crops?" He asked.

"Of course, but first we need to take care of you." She said.

"The missile?" He asked.

"Destroyed." She said.

"Jon?" He asked

"On his way out." She answered.

One of the androids came over to them with a medical kit in hand and started to work on Ben's wounds. Hannah held up a hand ever so slightly.

"I'll do that." She said. The android stepped back and a knowing eye would have seen a flicker of a smile on his face.

He might have thought. "It is good to have the humans here at last." But we will never know, for he had not been asked a question.

Sam walked over to Ben after he had his crew working on the brain reintegration at warp speed.

"Any instructions, Ben?" He asked.

"We will need a secure room build to house any problem androids or humans. Pierre will be the first resident." Ben said.

"Ben?" Sam said questioningly. Not really knowing if he should interrupt more.

"Sam." Ben answered.

"It is possible to reduce the power of an android body so they cannot escape a normal steel enclosure." Sam offered.

"Good. For problem people only though, just until we can get their head straight." Ben said.

"Sir. There heads are straight when we attach them." Sam said.

"Figure of speech, Sam. I mean when we get their thinking straightened out." Ben explained.

"Understood Sir." Sam said.

"Ben." Ben said.

"Sam, Sir." Sam replied.

"No. I mean call me Ben. We are in this together and equally." Ben told him.

"Very good. Ben." Sam said and turned.

"He almost looked embarrassed." Hannah told Ben.

"Maybe so. They are remarkable beings. I look forward to getting to know them better. Now, if you are finished taping me up, let's see about our crops." Ben told her.

Many eyes watched them leave the cavern, the humans smiled, the androids blinked their eyes and went back to work.

Chapter Fourteen

A national press conference opened with the president of the United States walking slowly and laboriously to the podium. The reporters were subdued as he reached for his notes. Nervously, he fumbled with the three-by-cards dropping a couple at his feet. An assistant quickly retrieved the cards and placed them in the appropriate order. The president looked for friendly faces in the packed room. His jaw twitched from his own stress and that showing on the faces before him. He looked at his cards and then up at the teleprompter. He began.

"Ladies and Gentlemen of the press, honored guests (in case there were some) and citizens. We are gathered here today under unprecedented conditions. Many, in our great nation, will not see the broadcast because of the wide spread devastation we have experienced in the last few days. Europe and the rest of the world have not escaped the sadness.

"For the record and as a background for those who may not know the events leading up to this moment in history, I would like to recap events as best I am able. Up until a short time ago, technology and biology had merged into the most amazing system of control which could be called neither technical nor biological.

"Many years ago, a man of extreme intelligence named Doctor Frank, devised a system that allowed the human brain to be preserved and active. At first, these were men and

women of renown, who were working on theories and
advances which would greatly improve the human race. Due
to the limited longevity of humans, many of these projects
were not carried to their full potential. With Doctor Frank's
system, these men and women could go on working in a
virtual world where they were monitored and their
discoveries catalogued for use in the real world.

"Over many decades and a few centuries, the system grew
and another was built in Europe. More complexes were
planned as nations developed an understanding of its
importance. The system became known as Preserved
Intellect.

"The care of the brains of these people were our number
one priority. Once a nuclear safe environment was prepared,
deep underground, the complex was moved there and
remains our most valuable national endeavor. The people of
the brains lived in a very complicated loop of time so that
they were not aware of their age. Their memory was modified
to reflect a recovery from what ever factor ended their life.

"We have always feared and Doctor Frank predicted that
eventually the brains would become aware and agglomeration
or clustering would occur. The danger in this event lies in the
conversations they would inevitability have between them.
The time loop would be discovered and there would be a
desire to escape their virtual world and cause insanity or
mass unrest among them.

"It does seem cruel, in retrospect, to imprison these people
in glass cylinders and deceive them with technology for our
own national needs. Nevertheless, over time, our Defense
Department became dependent on the brains. It seemed the
logical step to leap from allowing them to pursue their
intellectual goals, to the using of that part of their brain,
which was not so active, for other purposes. We did just that.
Once the Defense Department was successful, other programs
were tied into the Preserved Intellect system. Everything
from home computers to space vehicles were powered by the
brain complex. Needless to say, the two became irrevocably

intertwined.

"Without going into all the complexities, suffice me to say that there has been a breakdown of the system. Each complex, became so large from adding more and more brains, that a central brain was chosen and installed to facilitate order and continuity within the complex itself. This central brain had massive power and so was chosen very carefully for its intellect and emotional stability. At the time of the breakdown, two such central brains were in place. Others were planned for the near future.

"Because these brains enjoyed freedom to access the outside world, they were totally informed of world events and were aware of their station in the brain complex. They relaxed into the position and adjusted completely. The problem came when a series of events took place.

"Doctor Frank, being the author of the system, began to notice glitches in the system. These discoveries were noted when his emotion monitor spiked or elevated to a higher than normal level. It was little things that most people would have ignored. He had flashes of such things as his tie changing color. Once he started noticing these little things, he started playing with the system by changing his routine. There was an occasion when his virtual shadow did not change direction with him. The problem was fixed but the damage was done.

"Doctor Frank began an effort to contact his wife who died at a later time. For all either of them knew, she was in the real world and he in a virtual world. Then, his wife Doctor Ann Stein started noticing little things. In their virtual world, they had each lost the other. The did contact each other and a search for the real outside world insued.

"The third problem took place when a young computer hacker, whom we installed and called a searcher, contacted Doctor Frank. This completed the circle and matched some of the most brilliant minds in a battle against the most brillant minds of our day.

"Fourth and finally, the central brains became bored with

their isolation and contacted each other. An innocent series of chess games turned into a game of their own invention modeled on two strategy games molded into one.

"We were so confident of our choice of central brains and *the fail safes* built into the system, that we failed to notice when the central brains became unstable. They started using real property in their games. First, they were minor hits in unpopulated areas of the world. As the need for a greater challenge existed in their disturbed minds, the destruction became more serious.

"There, ladies and gentlement, is a brief history of an immense system we have come to rely on completely. Steps are now being taken to withdraw our technology from the brain complexes. The problem presents that the brains control all our systems. To withdraw without hesitation would throw us back into the stone age, if that ever existed in the first place.

"Be assured, civilization will survive to rebuild. We must not, however, be remiss in fully disclosing the full extent of the quandary we have forced upon humanity by our hastiness in using the brains of human beings without their knowledge. It should have been obvious to us that they would not be pleased if they discovered our misdeed.

"Lastly, a plan has already be executed to insure that humanity survives. For those of us left to deal with events as they occur, know that you have the support of your government and myself until the very end. That is all. Good Evening.

"No. I will not be answering any questions." He concluded.

"Mister President, the surgeons are waiting, we must hurry." An assistant said, talking fast.

"Yes, yes. I wish I could have been totally honest with the people. The poor devils do not know the half of their problems." President Bizmortee mumbled.

"I understand Mister President." The assistant consoled.

"We must avoid panic the truth would have caused."
The president said.

They walked together to Marine One which would take them to Air Force One. From there it would be a couple of hours to the facility where the president would undergo radical surgery. The end was near and it was of paramount importance that the president be in place to lead the free world after this disaster.

A squadron of top guns would escort Air Force One to its destination. Their unprecedented orders were to defend the president at all cost which included any hostile action by citizens.

Some top brass in the military knew the end was near. As human nature goes, they too would like to survive to live another day even if it was in another time.

Following Air Force One was deemed a hostile act, so it became necessary to fight to to eliminate pursuit. The generals wanted to know the location of the secret facility.

High above, battles were fought to keep the secret of the president's destination. Planes went down in corn fields, major cities and into rivers. Trails of flaming debris fell from the sky. Ordinary citizens looked to the heavens and knew that their brave fighting men were giving their lives to defend them. The media blasted scene after scene of a trail of destruction across the country. Little did they know that a struggle for survival of a different kind was going on above them.

The government had no plan to save the people. They were on their own. The government would never admit that important piece of information. They must always appear to be in control, even if it was the farthest thing from the truth.

A diversionary course was taken to prevent the military from projecting a destination. Finally, there was no pursuit. The escort planes were down to three from a group of sixty as the best fought the best. Air Force One landed with a nervous president onboard. The remaining three planes exploded into a ball of fire as the Secret Service set off top secret destruct signals. There action would hide the president's location from the world. The plane was lowered into an underground bunker and the area camouflaged to hid its arrival.

President Bismortee was ushered into a chamber to prepare him for surgery. He contact the Vice President, who was still in Washington with no idea of the extremities of the situation.

"I'm about to go under the knife, Jack. You have the nation. Take care of it." The president told him.

"There is a lot of stuff going on Mister President. It is a bad time to have your gall bladder removed." Jack replied.

"Tell my gall bladder that. You are the president now. Handle things the best you can. I have to go now before my surgeon's scalpel starts to rust." The president said and handed the phone to his assistant who nodded and left the room.

The vice president hung up the phone and rubbed his chin running his fingers through his hair with his other hand. He looked at the big desk of the oval office then turned to gaze out the window. For a split second, he stared into the nose cone of a nuclear missile. Then he was gone.

Sam came out to talk to Ben who was sitting near the water wheel. They had to yell to hear each other. That was why Ben sat there, to block out the noise of all the new voices and exclamation as new people discovered their new world and their new android bodies.

"We are ready to start on the last phase of the reintegration of the brains. Ah, humans." Sam said.

"Brains is fine Sam. I get the picture." Ben said.

"Ben, we have the last president of the United States in this ring. As you know, these are the last ones before the dark time. We may have some problems with them. The president, for one, is going to want to be in charge." Sam said.

"I know. I have been dreading him. What kind of man would leave his people to be destroyed and save himself?" Ben asked, knowing Sam would not have the answer.

"Not like Ben." Sam said. Maybe he did have the answer.

"He goes through the same orientation as the others. Use security if you must. There is no country for him to rule." Ben said with remorse in his voice.

Sam blinked then turned to follow his instructions. He saved the president until last and set the android strength to minimum. Sam stepped back from the android/president/human and waited for a reaction.

President Bizmortee looked around him. Memories came back.

"Take me to your leader." Bizmortee demanded.

"Very well. Right after orientation." Sam said.

"Get on with it." Bizmortee said.

Those assigned to the task attempted to explain to Bizmortee the circumstances and what was expected of him in this new world. He nodded, looked around the room and generally presented an air of impatience. Finally, it was over and he breathed a sigh of relief.

"Now, can we get on with it." He told Sam.

If an android had been programmed to roll his eyes, Sam would have done so then, but he was not so he turned and waited for Bizmortee to follow.

Sam walked smartly toward the water wheel. The president followed clumsily. Once he got his 'sea legs' he stood straight and tall in his android body which looked remarkably like his own. He would have preferred one a little younger but he did look presidential just like in the old days.

"This is Ben." Sam announced as if it was the final word.

Ben stood to his feet and gave a respectful handshake to Bizmortee. As expected, Bizmortee began to demand a full briefing and that proper accomodation be made for him.

"Sit down." Ben said.

"I will not sit down. I gave you some instructions, young man. I am accustomed to being obeyed." Bizmortee said.

"Sit down or I will have Sam here escort you to some adequate accommodations we have set up for some uncooperative arrivals. While you are in an android body, your strength is set to minimum. Sam has no such adjustment." Ben said. He had lost his sense of humor with this man. Bizmortee sat down, on a stump. Not the kind of seat he was accustomed to.

"What's the meanin……" Bizmortee started.

"I understand the position you held in your former life. You were in an office of great honor and respect. You had massive power at your command. I also understand that you left your people to die while you arranged to be preserved for the future." Ben told him.

"You cannot talk to me in this manner. I am the President of the United States." Bizmortee stated bluntly.

"You are the president of nothing. The country is gone. We are what is left of the human race. There are only a few of us trying to find order for our life. The fields are poisoned by your bombs and we must work very hard to make them fit for planting. We have an order of command which you may or may not understand. The androids understand and comply without question. Humans are the ultimate authority under the Mighty One. Androids know they are machines and respect us and our very wish is what they live for.

"Many human brains were preserved here and we have made every effort to respect and care for them. We have just completed the process of providing android bodies for all of them. We have oriented each one to their new surroundings. We have offered them a new life under our direction and supervision. It is not an easy thing to transcend from a virtual world to the real world.

"We have rules. Honesty not being the least of these. You will learn the others as you go along. Now, back to the order of authority. Humans born into their natural bodies have the final say. Androids are treated as equals except that they can never be human so they must be directed at times. Humans who have been incorporated into android bodies are under the supervision of humans born into their natural bodies. The reason for the last rule is that being several centuries behind reality can at any time cause emotional and mental
breakdowns. We will monitor everything completely so that everyone can have a happy and productive life. Do you understand?" Ben paused for his answer.

"They mentioned that in orientation. I think. I'm afraid I was not listening. So, I am not the president?" Bizmortee asked.

"You should have listened. It would have saved a lot of confusion for you. No. You are not the president." Ben said plainly.

"What can I do?" Bizmortee asked.

"You can advise me when I seek your advice. Otherwise, you can make a life for yourself. You have a healthy body and a strong mind. The world awaits." Ben said cheerfully.

"I can advise *you*? You are just a kid with too little experience for leadership. I would be better qualified." Bizmortee said as he stood to his full height.

Ben stood to his feet and stared Bizmortee straight in his android eyes.

"Mister Bizmortee. We have made every effort to help you understand. I think you do. I just burned up my best clothes getting rid of a nuclear bomb your people had hid here in this mountain. My mood is somewhat, shall I say, a little grumpy.

Unfortunately, we have no solution for stubbornness. So I will just tell you, I flipped the switch that awakened you. I can flip the switch to put you back to sleep. Look around you. It is your choice." Ben said.

"Well, I could take a small place." Bizmortee said.

"Plenty of room." Ben said.

"I could build a nice house." Bizmortee continued.

"We will help you." Ben said.

"I could have a garden." Bizmortee said.

"Acres of garden." Ben said.

"I get it. Cooperation. A new life. No country to run. Thank you young man. You are not a kid at all. I see why you were chosen to lead." Bizmortee went on.

"Well, before you get all speechee. I suggest you go meet Doctor Frank. He lives up on the hill there." Ben pointed to the distance.

"I'll do that. I'll do it now. If that is alright with you." He said.

"I really do not like this part of my responsibility. I hate having to be so threatening but we must have order. Now, if you will excuse me, that girl down by the stream is waiting for me to go check on our crops and to pick out a building site for our new home. We are getting married." Ben told him.

Sam somehow sensed the situation was resolved. He watched the two humans walk off toward the corn, now golden topped, then turned from his watchful post by the massive steel
doors and entered the cavern to put the finishing touches on the now empty brain facility. Everything would be sterilized and sealed. Then the massive enter doors would be closed. Only Ben would have the code to open them again. A code he would pass down to the next generation if he chose to do so. After these chores were completed, Sam would join the human race and help them rebuild. He would build a house for himself and perhaps do some traveling if the humans

permitted him to do so. It was up to them. Would this facility ever be needed again? The answer to that question was also up to the humans.

A baby cried in the night. Hannah was a mother. Ben stared in awe at the little boy. Sam blinked. Sam had a wife now who had served as midwife for Hannah, along with Ann, while the men walked the grass down to dirt in the front yard. Now they all stood at the crib Ben had made with his own hand.

"I wish androids could have babies." Sam said.

"Speak for yourself." Sam's wife said.

They all laughed together. The baby seemed to be laughing as well.

Outside it was very quiet. The frogs had multiplied to the point of being very loud at night. It was a clear night with stars abundantly shining over the family.

Doctor Frank and Doctor Stein, now just Ann Frank, walked up the hill toward their home. They gazed up at the stars and smiled at each other in between gazes.

"Do you like horses?" Doctor Frank said suddenly.

"Sure do. Did. Aren't they all gone? What brought this subject up? I haven't seen a horse since college. That was, oh, a few hundred years back." She said.

"I know where there are some horses. Hundreds of them." He paused to tease her.

"And when did you see these horses? Did you leave while I was asleep?" She asked.

"No. It was a few hundred years ago." He said. He was in no hurry and knew she was curious now.

"I give up. Where?" She asked.

"There is a cybergenics facility, not far from here,

where the embryos of all kinds of animals are stored. It was part of the Doomsday Project." He explained.

"Nice name." Ann said, sarcastically.

"Yes. Well. We could go there and bring the embryos out of hibernation. Once they mature, we could bring some back here. It would be like the old west." He said.

"That would bring our extended family forward a few centuries. Yes. I'd like to do that." Ann told him.

"It could be our second honeymoon and vacation. We could use a vacation. I think my last one was way too long ago. Let's tell Ben in the morning." Doc said.

"Let's wait a day or two. He will be busy at the house with the new mother and child." Ann advised.

"Of course." He said.

"Maybe we can talk a few cowboy minded androids into going along and help." Ann suggested.

"Good idea. Well, we are home. I am so glad. My feet hurt awful." He told her.

"Your feet can't hurt. They're android." She explained.

"Well, they would if they were my old feet."

Author's note

The human race is strong and resilient, yet fragile
in many ways, the least of which is not our ability to
think ourselves into a mess. I suppose we could make a
machine that processes information and is stronger than we
are, perhaps we already have, but they would not be human.

As machines cannot be made to be human, we cannot
make ourselves to be God. Boundaries exist for a reason. I do
not presume to know the extent of our mental ability to
invent, innovate or adapt. As a parent, I know that we are
often amazed with the reaching out of our children to learn
new things. Just as we teach our children their moral
boundaries, we must and should be aware of certain limits in
science which, if crossed, bring harm to us all.

About the Author

I was raised by poor parents. They were good people and I learned many things from them. My daddy has gone to heaven but my mom is still living, though quite elderly now. Most of my formative years were spent working on two different farms. On the first we grew cotton and corn as sharecroppers. Next, we managed a cattle and chicken farm. I suppose I can mark the time when I first started working full days in the fields with the first pair of shoes I bought for myself at age eight years old.

There have been many experiences to flavor my writing. I 'found my pen' while in high school writing for my English teacher who gave me no choice. Even then, the other kids would stop me in the hall to tell me how upset they were with what I said. I tried to tell them the teacher gave me the points to debate but that did not work. I realized then, the power words. They should be used wisely. There are close to ten novels around my desk or in boxes waiting for a publisher to discover. Maybe my wife will make a fortune off them after I'm gone. Regardless, I got to tell the story and that is what's important. They range from western to science fiction. I have stayed away from romance. What man understands that completely?

I'm about sixty years old, married, three children and nine grandchildren. Great grands are not far off. If I have been able to accomplish anything good with my writing, perhaps a smile from a reader, I must, and joyfully do, give God the glory for giving me the mind and heart to write. My wife is my best fan and helps me a lot with checking my books. There's no telling where I would be without her friendship and support. My what a journey life has been.

Book Two

"I'm not a great big tall oak tree,
but just a tender baby.
I cannot stand alone and tall
As I try you'll see me fall.

But with your help
I'll learn new things
And make you proud
In what life brings.

I need tender touch and care
And may cause you many tears.
But for almost any reason
I'll smile and sooth your fears.

I'll learn to love you
And you'll learn to love me more!

Harvest 2050AD

Milton J Southerland

Milton J Southerland
2441 Old Hwy 411 South
Chatsworth, Georgia 30705

Printed in the United States of America.

Voice in the Garden

Introduction

Mankind has outsmarted itself. They pried into the depths of the secrets of themselves. Scientists around the world discovered little pieces of the mystery of man. Each discovery was acted on without regard to other discoveries. They took their piece of the puzzle and decided that theirs was the ultimate answer to all the mysteries. It would have been prudent to conduct themselves as explorers. Then, the information could have been mapped and studied as a complete picture. However, the vanity of man would not allow logic to prevail. There was funding to be considered. The money people wanted results for their generosity. So, the cycle continued. Using painstaking techniques, a scientist would make an amazing discovery. Then it was as if all the safety protocols were turned off, caution was disregarded and the rush for results was on.

Finally, there was a breakdown in the fabric of mankind. By fabric, I mean the basic way mankind has always acted. The story would have been in history if history had not suffered a similar breakdown. It was concluded, in someone's mind in some past time, that mankind would be better off if they did not know their gruesome history. So it was rewritten to save our self-esteem. The fabric of the human code was also rewritten to rid mankind of those qualities that were undesirable. Ego drove the rich to reproduce themselves in their own image. Children were sculptured to reflect the perfect human to fulfill the ambitions of their parents. These magnificent humans knew they were superior to those unfortunate enough to be born without alteration. Their bodies were unusually strong so they could excel in sports. Their minds were uncluttered by morals. They pushed and shoved their way to success without regard for their fellow-man. Then there came a day when they reached the pinnacle of success. Parents were very proud but their children were virtually alone. The magnificent specimens had to turn on themselves to find another challenge.   An old, normal, scientist realized the mistake too late. Now, he must rebuild society with normal people. Where would he find them?

If this book should cause a tear? Or make you sad for the children? If this book has caused you to breath a prayer that we never stoop so low? Then the difficult task of ingesting the painful possibilities described within these pages was worthwhile.

I recommend this book for adults, only because some of the medical details may be a little tough on children. Otherwise, the language is clean.

**Chapter
1**

Chaos on Earth

The two handsome men took a break from their work to have an afternoon snack and a power drink. Friday was here so they kept up an old tradition of coasting through the last two hours instead of working. They were a fine-looking pair and were not surprised when two perfectly proportioned females looked them up and down as they passed by. Instinctively, the men flexed their muscles making their expensive shirts bulge against the seams. The women both fanned themselves with their hands and swished down the hallway. The men made the appropriate gestures of lust and desire and watched until the women turned a corner.

They were both more than six feet tall, weighing about two-hundred pounds each. Their weight would have been more if their parents had requested athletes. It was their good fortune, they considered, that their parents wanted financial wizards instead. One of the men was a half inch shorter than the other and so assumed a subordinate demeanor when they were together. The shorter one also had a gray eye that contrasted with his blue one. He had black hair. The combination made him distinctive in appearance which had always been a cause for discomfort to him. He had been spared because of the other qualities he possessed. After all, the flaws were only cosmetic in nature. His friend, however, was the picture of perfection. He had blond hair and blue-hazel eyes that seemed to change with his mood. Those eyes would twinkle at a funny story or soften over some sad pronouncement. The reaction had nothing to do with his feelings. Those feelings were cold and calculating. The designers had thought it appropriate to allow outward reaction to enhance conversation. The perfect one was named Bradford. His imperfect friend was called Jonathan.

"So, what do you have planned for the weekend?" Jonathan asked his friend.

"I plan to join a team to hunt for normals. Do you want to come along?" Bradford asked.

"No, I want to visit my parents this weekend. They are getting old." He replied.

"Are your parents normals?" Bradford asked.

"Yes, they are exempted, as yours are, so do not bring your hunting party that way this weekend." Jonathan said.

Parents that allowed the genetic engineering to proceed to its fullest potential were exempted for life. There were a few of them left around the world but time would soon overtake them and the world would be free.

"I like to visit my parents sometimes." Bradford said. "They are fun to study. It gives me an edge when I go on the sport hunts."

"If all parents were like mine, a world of normals might not be too bad." Jonathan said.

"Be careful, my friend. Someone might think that you had more flaws than that gray eye. That kind of talk is very unsafe and you know it." Bradford said.

"I thought a little casual conversation between friends would be all right." Jonathan said.

"Oh. Of course, it is all right. I was just teasing you, Jonathan. Do not think otherwise. You know we are the best of friends. Besides, I like your gray eye. It adds a little variety to the surroundings." Bradford said.

Bradford made a mental note, in that magnificent mind of

his, to keep an eye on Jonathan. It was possible that he was showing compassion for his parents. Compassion could lead to guilt when duty conflicted with those feelings. He smiled a perfect smile at his friend as he made his mental notes. Conscience did not hinder his thought pattern. He was void of guilt. The man he called his friend was indeed his friend to the extent that he could measure friendship. They worked together and sometimes played together. Should his friend show signs of being normal, Bradford would have no difficulty in changing his mind and making him an enemy.

Jonathan, on the other hand, looked at his friend and truly liked him as such. They had worked together since working on their doctorates together. Jonathan had a problem he would not discuss even with his friend. He loved his parents. They had done the best they could with him. He had received his genetic altering from a clinic of lesser standing than the one where his friend was engineered. Thus, the slight flaws that distinguished him. Love was not a convenient emotion to posses. Scientists had decided that the capacity to love hindered ones' ability to progress in the world. Love created baggage that must be cared for and considered in every decision. Yes, they decided, love was too cumbersome.

Jonathan sat with his parents in their living room. He had been able to provide a nice home for them, thanks to his financial wizardry. He owed it all to them. They had used their life's savings to alter his DNA so that he would have the mental edge. Now they were old and tired. Yet, there was a light in their eyes when they looked at each other. He saw the same light when they looked at him. They were proud of him. Their chairs sat at an angle toward each other with a small table between them. On the table there was a lamp and an old book that was out of print. They called it their Bible. If they had not been exempt, the book would have been confiscated and burned long ago. He picked it up and thumbed through the pages. It was torn here and there but the torn pages were carefully taped back in place. Almost all the pages had some passage underlined or a note beside it in the margin. He put the book down as certain lines came rushing back to his mind. His parents had taught them to him as a child. At times, the verses haunted him. At other times, they brought him peace.

On Sunday, his parents would have a few friends over for what they called church. A song would be sung from memory then one or the other would read from the Bible, as they called the book. Jonathan sat with them but did not participate in the service. He noticed the radiance on their faces and wondered at the ability to experience such joy. He listened as the passages were read and then explained. It was obvious that the old normals could not match his analytic abilities. They would stammer and flip back and forth to relate other passages to support their statements. He would have had a more organized approach to the whole thing. These were mere normals and they did the best they could. It was unfair to expect more from them.

Bradford was dressed in full body armor and a black helmet equipped with night vision. It was Saturday night. He and his friends had prepared all day going over maps and recent sightings of normals. They practiced with their weapons as if they needed practice but it was fun. He liked the roar of the automatic weapon he carried. They had lasers available but he like the sport of using the older weapons. The powder propelled bullets, at least, gave his prey a running chance.

In the alleys, the normals of all ages scurried like rats. They thought they were well hid by the darkness. The bounty on confirmed kills of normals was one thousand dollars a head. He had a payment coming up on his yacht so a few bounties would help with that and some fuel. He would need several weekends of hunting to fill the tank.

He looked through his rifle scope and the darkness turned green. Beyond the range of even his unaided eyes he spotted a movement through the lens. A pitiful, little normal ran across a narrow street and into a doorway. She knocked on the door but it did not open immediately. Bradford lined his sights and pulled the trigger. He spoke blissfully as his prey fell to the sidewalk. Not that he would have noticed, but the child was dressed in a dark head scarf over auburn hair. Her hair draped across a section of the sidewalk while the night breeze moved a single curl across her shadowed face. Her coarse dress fell shamefully above her knees revealing the bones of undernourished legs. She wore black high-topped shoes with black socks pulled up high. A modest girl in life, she was innocent in death. Her blood ran gently to the curb and neatly down the drain. Her face was serene. The startled eyes looked toward the darkness and saw nothing.

Bradford pulled the glove from one of her small hands and ran a pocket scanner across the finger tips. He dropped the hand as he looked into the scanner monitor. The palm of the hand slapped loudly on the sidewalk in the stillness.

The hunters moved on down the street and into the darkness of the run down buildings and rusted automobiles. When a safe time had passed, gentle hands picked up the girl and carried her to the belly of the city. There, her mother wept. Small children, who had known the girl, timidly touched the cooling flesh of their friend and cried. Two other women gingerly wrapped the small figure in the blanket she had slept under on long cold nights, leaving her face visible for one last kiss or touch or tear. The raggedly dressed men of the tunnels, beneath the city, carved a place in a wall to bury the dead.

Finally, they moved down the tunnels to a great metal door. There they shut themselves in for the night. In a corner, now too lonely, the mother could be heard throughout the night weeping for her daughter. A child coughed from the dampness and was consoled by her mother. The one candle they dared to keep burning reflected in the whites of eyes around the room. They must have slept at times but mostly the grip of fear kept them awake. They were normal and it was their cross to bear.

Bradford and his team had a good night of hunting. They had scanned fifteen by two in the morning and called it quits. The driver was called to pick them up. Their adventure had taken them deep into the old city. It had once been abuzz with normals but now it was rundown and the normals were down to a few thousand. Their driver was not happy when he finally got to their location. He was not a sportsman, and so, did not appreciate the fun the evening had brought them. He grumbled as he dodged abandoned cars on their way out of the hunting reserve. He said he was engineered to drive not to lead hunting safaris.

He turned a corner and smacked into an old man who was trying to hurry across the street. The old man carried a dirty blanket in his arm. Their hummer hit the man flat and he tumbled over the hood and into the windshield. Blood smeared the glass.

The driver cursed and got out after screeching to a stop. The body of the old man rolled to the pavement in front of the hummer.

"Now, I will have to spend my Sunday washing this machine." The driver complained.

"We will give you the bounty on this one. It is only right since you took him down." Bradford said.

The driver being properly compensated, dragged the body to the curb and dropped it rudely. They scrambled back into the vehicle laughing joyfully. Someone opened a bottle of bourbon to drink on their way.

Bradford got out at his house in the new city. The woman who met him at the door smiled and looked at him through sleepy eyes.

"Did you have a good hunt darling?" She asked.

"We took in sixteen thousand counting the one our driver ran down. It was a good night." Bradford bragged.

"That's good," She said sleepily, "now come to bed."

"I have to shower. It is dirty in the old city. You stay awake, now, you hear." He commanded.

She said okay but was fast asleep in a minute. Bradford came out of the shower and saw her sleeping. She had been engineered to be the perfect companion. By all appearances, the engineers were successful but her attitude could be tweaked a little.

"Oh well, I have to clean my rifle anyway." He said aloud but no one heard him.

Chapter
2

Jeb, the Old Scientist

Deep in the bowels of the old city a scientist worked over his test tubes and burners. Jeb was a scientist from the old school. He had made his discoveries in his day. Then, the new generation had taken those discoveries and corrupted their purpose. He taught at the university until the establishment got tired of his objections. His insistence that there were moral issues, to consider in research, slowed down progress. They told him. The arrant ways of society demanded results, not lessons in morality. There were games to win and exceptional men were needed to win them. The world economy required sharp minds to organize and perfect financial systems. Super soldiers were needed to keep the peace until the normals could be dealt with correctly. Yes, Jeb was a hindrance to progress.

Now, in his underground laboratory, he worked to save humanity. They did not know they needed saving. Jeb thought about a colony of ants he had read about once. They were strong and intelligent. Slaves were brought in to do the work. The slaves gathered food and dug tunnels. Smarter ants enjoyed their leisure and reproduced more of their kind. The tunnels the slaves dug were large enough for them but not large enough for their masters. Soon they could not leave the mound to capture more slaves to do their work. The masters were not worried for there were plenty of slaves to do their work. They did not have to leave. Then the slaves grew old and started to die, one at a time. The food supply became short. The masters tried to recruit more slaves but all the tunnels were too small. There had been no need for workers of their species because they had the slaves. So none were produced. Therefore, the master ants were not equipped to dig larger tunnels. They rested in their mound while the remaining slaves supplied their needs. It was enough for them to know that they were superior in intellect and strength. The slaves all died and the superior masters waited and waited until there was no strength to leave their mound.

Jeb was accompanied by four assistants. He knew them well for he had raised them from embryos. His assistants worked carefully in an immaculate chamber behind a sealed door in his laboratory. Their job was to watch over the children. The children were in various stages of development. None were of the super race. He had carefully read their history and chosen only those with no genetic engineering. They had been hard to find. Almost all the storage facilities had been cleansed of normals to make room for embryos of the altered generation. One had been forgotten. It was housed in the old city deep under abandoned buildings. The facility had an independent nuclear power source which he still used.

He could not defrost all the embryos at one time. The thought of thousands of crying babies gave him the hibby-gibbies. He respectfully tested each embryo until he found four unrelated, two males and two females. For years, he watched the world fall apart while he raised the four children. He schooled them completely. He told them the goal of genetic engineering and its pitfalls. He read history books to them with all the gruesome history of humanity. It was the real history. Now grown, they were at liberty to leave if they chose to do so, but none had left. He did not speak of reproduction to them. He would see if they chose a mate and let nature take its course. He had contact with an old couple who remembered the religion of his parents. They came to his laboratory on a regular basis to school his children. His was not an easy task. He was growing old and his joints hurt all the time. Day and night meant nothing in the depths where he worked but he kept an alarm clock set on twelve hour cycles so he could keep his children on a schedule of sleep and training.

Kayla interrupted his thoughts. She brought in a crying baby for him to check. He gently took the child and listened to its heart beat. Then he pushed lightly on its stomach.

"You have some air in your stomach little one." The old doctor laid the child on his shoulder and patted it gently. It made a couple of sounds and the doctor laughed. He sat down in an old rocking chair and continued to hold the child long after it fell asleep. Kayla watched for a while and went back to her work.

"You forgot your baby some place." Robert told her.

"Jeb has her. You know how he is with the children. He is their doctor and their mother." She said.

"Yes I remember. I think I like him better as a doctor. He can spank pretty hard." Robert said.

"He had to spank you to keep you from climbing out the ventilation ducts." Kayla laughed.

"You got me there." Robert answered.

They went up and down the line checking each incubation cell to make sure all the embryos were at the right temperature. They fed baby after baby and changed diapers. Their two partners, Kacie and Ben were sleeping now and would relieve them for the next twelve hours.

"I do not see how Jeb did all the work here before we were grown. He must have worked around the clock." Robert said.

"I wonder if he ever wishes that he had left us frozen." Kayla said.

"Not a chance. That old man has a heart the size of Montana. I wish he was not getting so old. I will miss him when he is gone." Robert said.

Jeb rocked the child gently in the old chair. He did not know if it was the rocking or the squeaking of the chair that quieted the children. The one he held rested quietly in his arms.

Jonathan watched a football game after their Sunday dinner. His mother might be a normal but she sure could cook. He loved to just sit and sniff the smells from the kitchen. She would sing some old song and Jonathan's daddy would pat his foot on the floor. She was singing an old song that Jonathan remembered. He hummed a few bars as she sang "Rock of Ages cleft for me, let me hide myself in the-e-e-e-e." My, how she could hold a note.

The football game was a battle of gladiator proportions. The ambulance crew hauled off athlete after athlete to the crowds loud cheers. One of the quarterbacks threw a pass from his end zone to the opponents five yard line where a sprint runner was waiting to catch it. He stepped into the end zone and scored. The score was high and looked more like a basketball score from the history books. Even basketball scores had increased to two hundred a game now. The commission had raised the baskets another six feet to keep the players from bumping their heads on them. There was talk of extending the football fields to half-again their present length. He got bored with the game and turned the set off. He kissed his mother and daddy then departed for his own house. It would be quiet there for he lived alone. He found genetically altered females too predictable. He wanted someone with whom he could share ideas. The women he met at work were only interested in being a good house partner. He wanted a friend.

He read part of a book then watched the evening news. Finally, it was time for bed. He found himself humming the tune his mother was singing as she cooked. "Rock of Ages, cleft for me. Let me hid myself in thee. Let the water and the blood, from thy wounded side..." He fell asleep trying to remember the story.

Bradford caught him at the coffee pot. Two female workers

were in the room so Bradford did his usual muscle flexing and smiling like a monkey with a banana until they left. Then he began a recount of his weekend.

"We bagged sixteen this weekend. Our total take was sixteen thousand dollars but we gave the driver one bounty for hitting a normal with the Hummer." Bradford recited.

"You seem very happy." Jonathan commented.

"Why should I not be happy? I have served the world community and paid some upkeep on my yacht." He said.

"I suppose you should be proud of yourself." Jonathan said with a little too much sarcasm.

Bradford did not notice. "My first kill was this scrawny little girl. She thought she was hid in a doorway but I got her with my first shot. Those normals keep forgetting about our night vision. Yes sir, I ripped her with my first shot. She twisted like a rag doll and fell like a stone to the pavement."

Suddenly, Jonathan felt nauseated. He excused himself quickly and dashed to the bathroom. He was bent over a commode when Bradford found him.

"Your not getting sick are you?" He asked.

Jonathan was pale from vomiting but shook his head. "I just ate too much of my mother's cake." He lied.

Bradford started to tell the story about the old man who stepped into the street at the wrong time but Jonathan had all he could take today.

"Just leave off the details." He snapped.

"Of course." Bradford said. "Anything you say old friend."

Bradford left the restroom and wandered down the hall to a door marked "Genetic Monitoring." He knocked and entered the room after a soft voice invited him to come in. She was a psychiatrist with a wall full of diplomas. Bradford talked sweetly to her forgetting momentarily his purpose for being there. She would not be fished into his net.

"You have something to report?" She said it as a question.

"Well, I do not know. Maybe." He stammered.

"What is it? You did not come in here to flirt with

me. I am sure. So, go ahead with what you have to say." She demanded.

Bradford wished he could back up in time and forget the whole thing. It was no longer possible to forget anything. The woman would make sure it was noted and analyzed to the fullest extent. He either had to tell his story or be interrogated by this computer in a movie star body. She adjusted her skirt.

"Well Bradford. Shall we talk?" Her lips matched her pink outfit.

Doctor Jeb put the baby in its crib and walked around the chamber looking at the sleeping babies. He visited the bedrooms of several children in various stages of maturity. They were fast asleep. Kacie and Ben were on duty now while the other team got some rest. They all had separate rooms on the opposite side of the laboratory. Ben walked out to the laboratory with the doctor.

"Doctor, how did we get in such a mess in the world?" Ben asked.

"That, my boy, is a short question with a very long answer." Jeb said.

"There were three ways to engineer humans: 1) Somatic cell manipulation involved adding genes to existing genes.   2) Cloning was making an identical human. 3) Germ line manipulation involved changing human genes of future generations. It was the most dangerous and the one chosen for the human race. It resulted in a person having DNA from two mothers and one father and was called mitochondria. It changes inheritable characteristics passed from one generation to the next. Scientists were already playing with eugenics but someone cloned a sheep in the early part of the century and set off a frenzy of activity.

"The practice of freezing embryos had already begun but it to had great moral implications. After all, who had the right to suspend another person's life for years then unfreeze them. Now it seems that the freezing of embryos will save the world. I am certainly happy to have you and the other children here with me. You look good for someone who was frozen at 196 degrees centigrade."

Ben laughed with Jeb. The last part was an inside joke down in the belly of the city. The children would never know their parents. They were long dead from old age or extermination. They had missed a very important part of their life. Jeb could not replace their parents but he could love them and do the best he could to teach them the truth.

"Ben, I have data from the new world that shows the population is decreasing rapidly. Much is due to the extermination but I factored that out. I do not know if it is that the new species just does not want the burden of children or that they have reached a point where the engineering has altered their ability to reproduce. I suspect it is the latter but they would be too proud to admit the truth. In any event, the earth will need normal people in the future. People with no moral compass will eventually kill themselves off. We must be ready." Jeb closed his eyes. He was very tired. He had been awake through most of two twelve-hour shifts.

"It is time for me to sleep, Ben. Look after the babies." Jeb said.

"I will sir. Just like you looked after me." Ben replied with a smile.

Ben watched Jeb get up and walk to his room. He moved slowly and slightly bent over. His hair had turned gray in the last few years. Ben remembered when it was black. Jeb laid down across his bed in his clothes. He would take a shower in the morning, time permitting. Tomorrow was church for the children. The old couple would come to bring milk and cereal and their Bible. Yes, he must get up early and get his shower now that he thought about it. He had forgotten the day of the week.

Bradford swallowed hard. He had never been speechless when with a woman until now. She clamped her lips together and then took out a mirror to check her lipstick. She uncrossed her legs and leaned toward Bradford. He knew then that he would tell her everything and make up some along the way.

"My friend Jonathan has been acting a little strange lately." He began.

"In what way?" She asked making it easy for him to continue.

"He seemed very uncomfortable when I told him about my weekend hunt. I believe the story made him sick. He vomited in the bathroom." He paused while she took down notes or drew a picture on her tablet. He heard it was a tactic used by cops and psychiatrist to make statements seem more important.

"Go on." She commanded.

"He spends his free time with his parents who are normals."

"Umm." She said. She flipped one shoe off onto the carpet. Bradford talked for an hour telling every detail he could think to mention about his friend. The woman had turned what he intended as a casual mention of his friend's problem into a detailed interrogation. He was defenseless before her. He knew all her comments and movements were calculated to break down his defenses but he could do nothing but her every wish. She made him wish he had much more to tell her. When it was obvious that he had told her everything, she dismissed him by rising to her feet and putting her shoe back on her foot crossing her leg across her knee as she did so. The calm and always in control Bradford ran into his chair as he turned to leave. The doorknob seemed very complicated to him as he fumbled to open the door. The woman smiled at his back as he left her office. "Like putty in my hand." She said aloud.

**Chapter
3**

Jonathan's Troubles

When Jonathan next saw Bradford he sensed that something had changed between them. Bradford hesitated to make eye contact and when he did for a moment, he turned away quickly.

"What's wrong old friend?" Jonathan asked.

"Nothing is wrong. I have a lot of work to do. Do I have to be cheerful all the time?" Bradford barked.

"Well, you usually are cheerful but everyone has a right to an off day. I will leave you to your work." Jonathan said.

Jonathan pulled his keyboard closer and concentrated on his monitor. He was doing a stock comparison chart for the boss. A woman dressed in pink came wondering through the office. Normally, Bradford would have been on his feet introducing himself. Jonathan had seen the woman around but never in the break room or at any office functions. She bounced up and down as she walked causing her blonde hair to wave like the tail of a horse. She stretched the fabric of her skirt with each step, surely testing the seams. She walked the long way around the office allowing the whole staff to admire her beauty. Jonathan worked his keyboard manipulating the chart skillfully. He reached for one of his many reference books and there she was standing in the door to his cubicle. She stood with feet apart and hands folded in front of her body.

"You must be Jonathan. I have heard a lot about you. I am

the company counselor. My name is Matilda Peeks." She said extending one of her hands.

Jonathan took her had and felt a chill run the full length of his spine. He could not have explained why he felt the way he felt. The woman was perfectly nice. She smiled up at him with moist pink lips but Jonathan had the uneasy feeling that she was looking down at him. He pulled his hand away a little too quickly. She smiled at his quickness and put one hand on a hip then changed her expression to mock pouting.

"I am sorry, was my hand cold?" She asked.

"No, it was warm. I did not mean to pull away so abruptly." He lied.

Bradford sat across from Jonathan's cubicle and could see only the woman's back. He attempted to do his work but his eyes kept wondering back to the pink clad beauty. He almost felt sorry for his friend but it was not a feeling he was capable of having. He, perhaps, felt fear which still plagued him at times.

"We should talk in my office sometime. Would tomorrow be a good day for you?" She asked.

"I have a lot of work to do. I appreciate your kindness and I do not want to be rude but I must decline your invitation." Jonathan told her.

"I think we should talk. I am afraid I must insist. It is my job, you see." She said. The smile had left her lips but remained in her eyes. Jonathan thought back to the orientation given him when he came to the company. She waited, knowing the working of the human brain. She knew he was sorting through memories tucked away in the far reaches of information. Information he had filed away thinking it would not be needed.

Jonathan remembered. "Company counselors are to be respected for their authority over all company employees."

"Of course, I will be there. What time is good for you?" He asked.

"Oh, just drop in at your convenience. My schedule is very

flexible." She said. The smile had returned to her lips. She did a smart left turn and left the work area. Jonathan listened as her heels announced her departure. Then he looked over at Bradford who had turned toward the window with a book on his knees. Jonathan leaned back in his chair and faced the wall. There were other memories he must retrieve. He sat with his eyes shut. Finally, a startling memory of information jumped to the front of his brain. "In any instance of suspicion that an employee is showing characteristics of being normal, he or she is to be reported at once to the company counselor. Any member proven to be normal will immediately be dismissed from the company and their parents will forfeit their exemption."

"So that is where Bradford took off to." He thought.

Jonathan finished his project and transferred it to his boss's computer. He realized he must get to his parents before the police. He turned to Bradford with the biggest smile he could muster.

"I have to turn in some dirty laundry and pick up some clean. I may take the afternoon off if anyone is looking for me." He told him.

"Sure buddy." Bradford said with a half-smile.

Jonathan grabbed his coat from the coat rack in the corner of his cubicle and left the office. As the elevator door closed, Matilda opened her door and watched it close. She went back to her office where she watched Jonathan get into his car and speed away. She smiled to herself. They all acted the same way. She knew Jonathan would try to warn his parents. His normal tendencies were obvious from their conversation so she had immediately notified the police to pick up his parents. She filed a report that their exemption was canceled. The police called her with the news that Jonathan's parents were not to be found. Their home was empty. She ran her hands down the front of her suit jacket. These cases always were exciting.

Jonathan pulled into his parents driveway. He had a key to

their house on his key ring. He burst into the door. His mother was not in the kitchen, her usual place. His daddy was not in his chair next to the Book. He searched all the rooms and the basement then went into the back yard. They were not here. On the kitchen, next to the bread box, he found a list of phone numbers. He tore off the list and stuffed it into his pocket. If his parents returned, they would not get a chance to make any phone calls. Then, he noticed the answering machine flashing and pushed the play button. The message was eerie.

"This is the police. You are to report to the nearest police station upon your return. You are aware of your obligations." The machine went silent.

Jonathan went into their bedroom and pulled a suitcase from the closet. He quickly dumped the contents of several drawers into the suit case. Then, he went to the bathroom and got the dental items there. He was sure he had forgotten a lot but it was the best he could do. He rushed to his car and threw the suitcase in the backseat. He knew he could not go to his house so he stopped at a store and picked up some personal items for himself. At the ATM he withdrew the maximum allowed. He knew his cell phone would be monitored so he stopped at an Internet café to call the people on his list. He recognized them as people who had attended the church services at his parents home. None would admit to knowing the whereabouts of his parents. They were obviously protecting a secret. In desperation, he called one of the numbers back and told his story. There was a long silence on the other end. Jonathan waited.

"I will be waiting for you at the edge of the old city." The voice said and gave Jonathan a street corner.

Jonathan looked out the window of the café as the conversation ended. A police car waited out front. He gave one of the students a twenty to bring his car to the back alley then he went out the delivery door in the back. The student casually got into the silver Porsche driving straight down the street. He was almost out of sight before the police car took up the pursuit. They had not been fooled for long. The student changed gear and made a screeching right turn. He really liked this car. He made a left at the next corner then two rights bringing him to the alley behind the café.

He slid to a halt in front of Jonathan. "You better boogey, the cops are on the way."

Jonathan slid into the now vacant seat. "Thanks." He yelled over the roar of the engine. He wound the engine tight in first gear leaving two long marks on the pavement. Then he disappeared around the corner. He crossed the street where his car had been parked driving in the opposite direction the student had taken. He slowed to the speed limit and watched for police cars. He could not let one get behind him to read his tag. He drove toward the old city and the address he had been given.

It felt strange to be on the run. He had hidden his feelings all his life knowing the consequence to himself and his parents if he was revealed. He knew, now, that his parents had altered his mental capacity and left his other features intact. Emotionally, he was a normal.

An old gentleman stood on the street corner with a grocery bag in his arms. He had a walking cane hooked over his arm. He appeared to be resting. Jonathan shifted gears and swung into the side street past the old man. The old man did not move immediately. Jonathan sat in the car wondering if the man had seen him. Then, the old man shifted his grocery bag to one arm. He retrieved his walking cane from its resting place and leaned heavily on it. Slowly, he turned down the side street, hobbling past the silver Porsche. He looked at the tinted window on the driver's side. Jonathan rolled down the glass. The old man nodded and walked to the passenger side. He got in surprisingly fast.

"Drive straight down this street and turn when I tell you. Do not waste time, now, we must hurry." The old man said.

They left the boundary between the old and the new. Only

the ruins of the old city lay ahead. This was Bradford's hunting grounds. Jonathan swung from side to side going around abandoned cars and piles of trash. Deep into the heart of the old city they drove. The old man called out instructions well ahead of every turn. He was mentally sharper than he appeared. They finally came to the end of what looked like a dead end street. The old man, more agile now, scrambled out of the car and opened a roll-up garage door. He motioned for Jonathan to drive through then closed the door behind them.

"You will need your lights now." The old man said.

They drove down into a parking complex. Then went round and round until they reached the bottom deck. The old man got out and opened another garage door and told Jonathan to park his car inside. The old man picked up a couple of old brooms and gave one to Jonathan. Then they started sweeping out the tire tracks in the dust on the floor. After the old man was satisfied that they had gone far enough, they walked back to where the car had been hidden.

The old man opened a squeaky steel door and motioned Jonathan inside. They descended further into the belly of the old city, down metal stairs laden with rust. The old man produced flashlights, for there was no sunlight here. The old man carried his cane like a club, apparently not needing it to walk. He stood straighter as well. Jonathan had good ears, better than the old man it seemed. A familiar sound registered on his brain. He stopped and motioned for the old man to do the same. There it was again. He recognized that voice.

"Rock of Ages, cleft for me, let me hid myself in the-e-e..."

"It is the air ducts." The old man explained. "Sound travels down here sometimes."

They walked until they came to a large steel door. The old man rapped on it with the side of his fist. An ancient man wearing a white lab coat opened the big door. They entered and the door was closed behind them. The room they entered was well lit so they turned off their flashlights.

"Hello son." A voice said behind him. He turned to see his

mother holding a child.

"Hello mother. It is good to see you." Jonathan said.

She walked to him. Instead of hugging him as she often did, she handed him the baby she held. "Hold him." She said. "I have another one that needs feeding."

The old man in the lab coat directed Jonathan to an old rocker.

"Here, young man, you can sit here with the baby."

Jonathan sat down. The natural thing seemed to start rocking in the old chair. It squeaked with age and hours of use. The baby wiggled to a comfortable position in his arms. The old man smiled down at him.

"My name is Jeb. I run this facility." He said.

"Are you farming babies?" Jonathan asked.

"Just gathering in the crop my boy. Just gathering in the harvest." Jeb said and ran his knotted fingers through his shock of gray hair.

Jonathan looked down at the trusting child. He pulled it a little closer and watched its movements. Jeb had turned to talk to the old man who brought Jonathan to him.

"He was on the run. I had to bring him." The old man told Jeb.

"You did right. I will fill him in later. Right now he is getting his orientation." They turned to the young man in the rocking chair. The young man watched the baby's every move. It was holding onto Jonathan's finger. Jonathan had always thought of normals as being flawed but he was looking at perfection. A small human with great potential, just as it was meant to be.

The baby went to sleep and his mother came to put it to bed. Jeb took Jonathan on a tour of the chamber and the rows of babies. Then to the rooms of the children in various stages of maturity. It was almost too overwhelming.

Jeb explained the history of the facility and how it had

been abandoned and forgotten. Jonathan began to wonder what else might have been abandoned under the old city.

"There used to be a hospital in the old city," Jeb said, all the research facilities sort of spread out from the hospital."

"Then there could be more of these places?" Jonathan asked.

"There could be about anything under the old city. Research went crazy after Dolly was cloned. They all had their own agenda. I have not had time to search all of it, just this facility. The tunnels go everywhere. If we did not have to eat, we could stay down here indefinitely." Jeb said.

"How do you get food?" Jonathan asked.

"The church people buy extra and bring it to the children. It gets more difficult all the time. They must sacrifice their own diet to provide enough for the children. We keep it all very secret. The government expects the old normals to die out in a few years, so they mostly just let us be." Jeb said.

Chapter
4

Belly of the Old City

Jonathan's mind was engineered to be a financial wizard. He was also a curious person. Jeb had a small library in his laboratory. He used his improved mind for another purpose now. For weeks, Jonathan rocked babies and read books. There were books concerning the embryo storage market which was wide-spread and very competitive. Many of the books were on DNA manipulation. He found, also, that cryonic suspension was a large industry. People had themselves frozen for various reasons, for a fee. The companies were suppose to thaw them when a cure for their particular disease was found. In the case where the head only was frozen, the hope was for cloning to be perfected which would provide them with a new body. Researchers theorized that the brain held the only useful material needed for a new life. He read reports of black market cloning where people were grown for spare parts. Various parts were removed while they were held in suspension.

Jonathan's emotions, which had been bridled for years, now flooded his whole personality. He wept openly as he read about embryos being stored in straws at the fantastic low temperature of 196 degrees centigrade in liquid nitrogen. The whole country seemed to be engrossed in nanotechnology. If money could buy it, researchers could find a way. They must have been swimming in grant money from organizations and individuals where the desire to extend life was strongest. A rich millionaire once stated that he would gladly give his fortune for just a few more minutes.

Armed with new knowledge, Jonathan realized that he lived in a world gone berserk. The madness started with the alteration of the food supply. Animals were given hormones to increase production. Cows must give more milk. The advantages of a child drinking plenty of milk as they grew up has been breed into peoples minds for years. So they drank hormone enriched milk and got fat. The real taste of food was soon forgotten and replaced with a palate that desired food from a can or freezer. The population became out of shape and mentally sluggish. They were no longer acceptable so genetic enhancement of the depleted human race seemed like the logical next step. The rush to alter the entire human race was not well thought out and certainly not a logical step. Greed was the motivation in almost every instance. True, there were noble people who wanted to cure disease but when a breakthrough was obvious, the new technology was appropriated for rapid marketing and quick money.

The government was not innocent. They needed soldiers with advanced abilities. A soldier who would not break under interrogation could be trusted with better information to carry out his mission. Marksmen needed enhanced eyesight. The soldiers became a test case. The government was not above starting a little war to test their subjects. The success of the experiments was unquestionable, so the government dumped mega-money into genetic research.

Jonathan threw a book across the laboratory sending it crashing into a wall. The baby he held jumped and opened its eyes. Jonathan patted the child and looked around the room. He had attracted the stares of the staff and his mother. Jeb walked to the book and picked it up. He gently put it on the shelf where it belonged.

"Sorry about that." Jonathan apologized.

"Never mind that boy. I've thrown a few of those books myself. I have most of them memorized now so getting away from the information is not so easy anymore." Jeb said.

"I have a photographic memory. The pages run through my head like a fast-moving slide show." Jonathan said.

"A blessing and a curse." Jeb said solemnly.

Jonathan got up and carried the baby into the chamber and put it to bed. He returned to talk to Jeb. Jeb raised himself up from his test tubes to listen.

"There are things I can do to help but you have managed for a long time without being discovered. I do not want to do anything that might jeopardize what you do." Jonathan began.

"Whether you did anything or not, we are always in danger of being discovered. Do what your heart tells you." Jeb told him.

"I thought of setting up a defense guard in case the hunters come below. I would like to recruit the street people. It would give them purpose. I cannot just let them get shot down up there." Jonathan explained.

"I am an old man. Twenty-four hours is not enough to complete my daily work. I must test every embryo before thawing them. There are so many. Sometimes, I am tempted to rush the process but each one is a unique life. I must be patient and hope I live to complete my work. My assistants are almost ready to continue the work if I die. Do what you can. We need your expertise." Jeb said.

Jonathan nodded. He knew what must be done. His first step must be to explore the underground. There were things he would need. He needed at least two assistants to help him get his tasks started. He turned to Jeb.

"Do you know any retired computer specialist? I want to set up a control room to monitor our defenses." Jonathan said.

"The man who brought you in is named Peter. He will know the right people." Jeb said and turned back to this work.

Jonathan knew that Jeb did not mean it as a dismissal. He

was just in a race against time. At his age, he should have been in an overstuffed chair reading his favorite book. Lives existed at 196 degrees centigrade and he must save them. The cry of every child proved him to be a hero. If mankind survived, Jeb would be remembered.

Jonathan went to his mother to explain that he would be away for a while. She indicated that she understood.

"We will be here. There is no other place to go." She said.

The belly of the city was like a rusty old ship. Water dripped into the tunnels here and there. Any sound seemed to echo down endless distance. Jonathan carried a flashlight and several extra batteries. Down tunnels he trudged carefully. He opened large metal doors to see what was inside. Occasionally, he climbed up a rusty staircase to the street to look out. Laboriously, he worked out his surroundings. On one of his visits to the streets above, he found an abandoned store that had sold computers and parts in the past. The machines were outdated but would be useful. He could not carry all the technology he would need, so he noted the place and continued exploring. He found the old hospital and wondered through its many corridors. Then he saw what he needed. He had stopped to rest when he noticed them and a plan formed in his mind. There were security cameras in all the halls and waiting areas. He kept looking and found the security office with its bank of monitors. He had a complete system right here and so would not have to build one from scratch. He was excited when he returned to laboratory. Everyone was interested in his discoveries. It was like their first strategy session.

Jonathan left to explore the more immediate area. He found what he was looking for one level up. There was a secure room that he could use for a command center. A room off to one side would serve as his living quarters. There were several rooms across the tunnel that could be cleaned up for those who were recruited to help him.

The hunters did not usually come out in the day time so

Jonathan found an abandoned building and sat down to watch the streets. He was back in the shadows so he would not be easily seen. He, too, was hunting but not for the purpose of killing. He was looking for people to help him. The first day was fruitless. He saw people in the distance but could not tell anything about them. The second day he sat scratching his, now long, beard with his fingers. The beard was to be part of his disguise. He kept his hair trimmed neatly but wore a hat he had secured from an old store. The hat looked good he thought after he got the layers of dust cleaned off. Sunglasses were necessary because of the light that seemed so bright after spending so much time below.

He was remembering the books he had read and wondering about his old friend Bradford and the woman in pink. His life had changed overnight. He was the hunted now. His friend would be his adversary. The woman would not forget about him. He knew she would be alert to any trail he left. So far, he had stayed out of sight. His car had not been moved. He had not made any contacts with the new city people.

Then, he saw her. She went into an old clothing store across the street. The clothes had been rummaged through several times and were scattered about the store. She was short and slim. A toboggan hid most of her hair. Black strands escaped and hung around her ears. She was dressed in black which would have made her almost invisible on the streets at night. Today, though, she was either careless or deviant by walking around in broad daylight. Jonathan watched her move and decided that she was not careless.

Jonathan walked boldly across the street and entered the store. The woman was not in sight. He looked through some of the clothes as if that was his purpose for being here. He walked to the counter where items would have been paid for in bygone days. He leaned over the counter to look behind it and stared into the mussel of a Smith and Wesson .32 revolver. He looked beyond the weapon into the most beautiful eyes he had ever seen. She held the gun level and steady. Jonathan backed up two steps and stopped, waiting for her to instruct him. She came around the counter and walked behind him. Jonathan felt himself being frisked thoroughly for weapons. She was not shy at all. "You do not look like someone who would have to come here to shop." She said in a quiet feminine voice.

"I am not shopping for clothes but I am shopping." He said.

"Okay, I'll bite. What are you shopping for?" She asked.

"People." He said. She raised the weapon and pointed it at a point between his eyes.

"I am not a hunter." He assured her.

The weapon lowered slightly. She backed up and felt for a stool with one hand. She sat down.

"So, talk." She said.

"Could you put the gun away? It messes with my thought pattern." Jonathan asked.

"Sure. I can put it away but I can get it again very quickly." The woman put the weapon in her belt in easy reach.

Jonathan began his story with his parents and went through his betrayal by his best friend. She listened without interrupting. Finally, he was silent.

"So, why are you here?" She asked.

"To fight back. My parents are normals. I have new friends who are normals. It is time for us to defend ourselves." He said.

"I am for that idea. We better go get you a gun though. You cannot be much of a general without a gun." She said and walked past him and headed down the street.

He hesitated a moment and then followed her. She waited on a corner up the street. When she saw he was following, she turned on her heel and swished down the side street. Occasionally, she looked back and flashed a beautiful smile over her shoulder. She led him several blocks further into the city and into a store that appeared to have been a pawn shop. He saw no weapons. She pulled on one end of a display case and revealed a hidden room. It was relatively clean. He entered and she pulled the panel closed. She stood to one side and smiled her nice smile at him. There were several rows of what would be considered antique weapons and a shelf loaded with real bullets.

Jonathan picked out a shoulder holster and strapped it in place. Then he picked up several weapons until he found one that suited his grip. Then he found another weapon he liked. It was an open front holster with a sawed-off shotgun inside. The belt had room for twenty-four rounds. The weapons would be a load to carry but he was strong and felt comfortable carrying them.

He looked at the woman. "There is just one thing. I am in charge. I will not tolerate insubordination. We will be against superior forces who are genetically enhanced." He paused.

"Where to General?" She asked. She was apparently full in agreement.

"First, we pack up some of these weapons and ammo." He said.

"I spotted some backpacks that will help." She said and dashed out of the hidden room. She was back shortly with two sturdy canvas packs to carry the extra weapons. They walked silently down into the bowels of the city. Jonathan stopped and turned to face her.

"There are some very important secrets down below. You must promise me that you will keep and protect those secrets." He said earnestly.

"Yes, General." She said.

"Please, do not 'yes general' me on this one. Lives are at stake and I must have your promise." He said.

She looked hurt and told him sincerely. "I have lived in the old city for a long time. These people have been my people for just as long. I would not betray them."

"Thank you. I am sorry to question your sincerity." He

replied.

She lightened up again and smiled at him. "Lead on General." She said.

Jonathan turned and led the way down the stairs and many tunnels of the old city. The stairs groaned and squeaked with each step. Their movements echoed down the damp corridors. He heard the steps behind him and smiled. He found comfort in knowing that this woman walked behind him.

He took her to his recently acquired command center. She looked all around and picked out her a room.

"Sorry. That room is mine. I will be closest to the door in case of trouble." Jonathan said.

She looked further and took the one straight across from his.   "We will get them in a crossfire." She said.

"What is your name?" He asked.

"Charlie Grace." She said.

"Jonathan." He said.

She stuck out her hand and he took it gently. There was a bond established as their eyes met and held.

"We may die, you know." He said. "This is the path I have chosen."

"You do what must be done. I got your back." She said.

He watched as she chose weapons for her personal use. He knew then that she would keep that promise with her very life.

Charlie told Jonathan that she had a brother about twenty who would help them. They lived together in the lower level of an old hotel. She said she had to go get some of her things and she could bring him along.

"Do you trust him?" Jonathan asked.

"With my life." She replied.

"That's good enough for me. I will go with you. There are some computer parts I would like to start hauling back here. First, I must show you what we are protecting." He said.

They went down one level where Jonathan knocked on the big metal door. Jeb opened the door part of the way to see who was there. He hesitated when he first saw Charlie.

"She is okay." Jonathan told him.

Charlie walked into the laboratory then Jonathan led her into the chamber to see the children. She stopped at each one. Sometimes, she touched a small finger or fixed a blanket. She went into the play room where most of the older children were being attended by his mother. Charlie sat down on the floor and helped a child fit blocks into place. Jonathan left her with the children and rocked one that was fretful. Jeb came up with some soup for supper so they ate their first meal for the day. Charlie was silent during the meal. She was ready to go when Jonathan rose to leave. She walked to the command center and into her room. She laid down on the floor and went to sleep without saying a word. Jonathan understood her silence. They sleep the night through. Jonathan stirred in the command center and heard a weapon being readied for use.

"It's me." He told Charlie.

Charlie put the weapon away and stretched out the kinks from sleeping on the floor. Both of them strapped on their weapons and headed toward the hotel to get her brother. His name was Raleigh. He was a husky young man with unruly hair and obviously underfed. He had a scar on one cheek compliments of the hunters. Introductions were made then Raleigh offered them some breakfast, a can of peaches for each of them. Jonathan was silent while Charlie told her brother what was up. He drained the juice from his peaches.

"It is about time." He said and got to his feet. He waited for Jonathan to rise.

"Alright. I guess we are ready to get started. We have a command center to build." Jonathan said, getting to his feet.

He headed toward the computer store with his new recruits in tow. He made it a rule to not cross open streets unless absolutely essential. They would go down a level and find a way to cross underground to the other side.

The day was spent hauling computer parts to the command

center. The work was tiring. On one of their return trips with a load, Peter was waiting for them.

"Jeb said you needed to see me." He said.

"Yes sir. I need a computer networking man to hook up our system. Tell him it is old stuff but still functional. He should be single or be willing to bring his wife and live here from now on." Jonathan said.

"I think I can find a man. It may take a week or two for him to make the move. He will have to sell his house to have money for later." Peter said.

"I understand. We have to run a lot of cable, so two weeks should be about right." Jonathan told him.

Peter left thinking that he was glad he decided to trust Jonathan. He was an answer to their many prayers. Raleigh had a friend who lived alone in another building near the hotel. He got permission to recruit him for their team. They were four strong now.

For two weeks, the four of them hauled in computer equipment and mounted cameras in the streets. They ran cable for the cameras so that they could be tapped into the command center. In some cases, it was a matter of tracing phone lines and using those. The first phase being completed, they strung spot lights where there were none in the streets and wired in others. All this work was just preparation for the real mission which was to protect the area around the baby facility.

Jonathan went to the fringes of the new city one day and purchased a wireless laptop computer. He used it from a remote location away from their command center. He did not want to be traced back to the children. Each time he used the laptop for thirty minutes, he changed locations. It was good that he did for on more than one occasion he saw the police check out places he had transmitted from.

"So," he thought "they were watching for him. They knew he was in the old city but that was a lot of ground to cover."

Once he realized this, he hopped all around town and

stayed for only ten or fifteen minutes at a time. During these transmissions he managed to hack into a government computer and increase the elderly pensions by 5 percent. It would give his friends more money to buy food for the children. He sent a news release to the newspaper to announce the happy event. The politicians were not happy with the increase but were quick to see the advantage of taking credit for the raise.

He transferred his savings to another bank under a fictitious name. He then went to that bank and withdrew most of the money. He now had a bankroll for necessary purchases.

The computer man went to work as scheduled. He tied in all the street monitors and lights to a control panel and the computer monitors. They were no longer blind to activities on the streets above. The lights would only be used in emergencies.

Jonathan acquired motion censors so they could track movement after dark. He equipped each of his recruits with a two-way radio complete with earpieces. Raleigh became his best recruiter. He knew a lot of the street people. He had provided many of them with food when they had none. Charlie brought in a friend of hers. She was strong and totally loyal.

"You have to stop running off alone with that computer of yours. I want to be with you from now on. If they capture you, they will extract our location, one way or another. We need you and besides I promised to watch your back." Charlie told him.

"Okay. I did not look at it that way. From now on, we are a team. Capture is not an option. Agreed?" Jonathan said.

Charlie knew it might mean one of them having to shot the other. She nodded solemnly.

"Capture shall not be an option." She repeated.

Chapter
5

A Sick Baby

Jeb looked into the incubator. The embryo was not strong enough to complete the process. He shook his head. It would not be the first one he had lost but it never got easy. He could rock a full term baby in his old rocking chair and comfort them. He could not even touch the embryo for fear of contamination. He had watched them develop many times and knew that this one, although healthy, was getting weak.

Kayla saw his concern and walked to his side. She, too, had become expert at reading the signs of trouble. She, too, had seen them die. To her, they were all family. They rested for years in the same freezing temperatures. They were all from another generation and would be part of the elderly generation if they had been born normally.

"Robert and I want to get married." She suddenly blurted.

"I thought it was Robert's place to tell me that. You know, like asking for your hand and such." Jeb said.

"Well it is 2050 and the occasion seemed right." She said.

"What is the occasion?" He asked.

"I want to have a baby and I want to be married when it happens. I am also very much in love with Robert." She told him.

"You have things in the right order." He said.

"Then 'yes' is the answer?" She asked.

"Yes. Yes is the answer." He replied.

"What about having the baby?" Kayla asked.

"That is up to your husband and the Good Lord, not me." Jeb argued.

"I know that Jeb but I want it to be this baby. The one you are worried about living." Kayla told him.

"So, that is the 'right occasion' you were referring to."

"Yes."

"The embryo does not have very much longer before it will be damaged. You would be saving its life." Jeb said.

"And it would be making my life much fuller." She said.

"You are a wonderful young woman. I think of you as my daughter. I am very proud of you." She hugged him then and he almost wept.

"Now, get on, you have plans to make and I have to find a preacher." Jeb said.

She ran to Robert and told him the news. He hugged her then released her quickly when he saw Jeb watching them. He walked over to the doctor and shook his hand.

"Thank you sir." Robert said.

"It is a tragic time to raise children but they are our future. You have a grave responsibility and I know you will do well." Jeb said.

Jeb went back into his laboratory and picked out his book on implanting embryos. It would be the first one brought to maturity without his watchful eye. Normal was such a wonderful and beautiful word. The embryo could not wait so the wedding ceremony was scheduled for two days away. Charlie found a wedding dress for Kayla and a tie for Robert. Kacie and Ben served as bridesmaid and best man. Jeb gave away the bride.

Jonathan stood honor guard with his recruits. They stood at attention in military fashion with weapons holstered. One person monitored the command center, two more guarded the doors. The operation for the implantation was carried out immediately after the wedding. The embryo could not wait any longer. Both occasions were cause for celebration so they used some of their valuable supplies for a reception.

**Chapter
6**

Street Fight

On a dark Saturday night, the hunters came to the old city. They had to go deep into the city to find their prey. The game was thinning out.

Bradford was in overdrive. He had been out of the hunt for several weeks. After the thing with his friend Jonathan, he lost heart for the hunt. Matilda, the psychiatrist, started watching him to close. It was time for him to show that he was okay. A good hunt would do the trick.

They entered the old city at sundown. The streets were ghostly and quiet, except for the breeze blowing things around. Paper rolled down streets, signs moved on rusty hinges. The moon was taking its rest. Their driver took them slowly through the rubble. As usual, they were in full body armor and wore their night vision goggles. There was no movement in the city.

Bradford told the driver to stop the vehicle. He got out with a teargas rifle which had several canisters attached. If the prey would not come out voluntarily, he would just have to flush them out. He fired into a building across the way. His team waited with weapons ready. Nothing happened. He fired into another building and another. The smoke filtered out of the windows along the street. The tactic worked. Two normals came rushing out of a building coughing and rubbing their eyes. The hunters took aim and dropped them before they got half way across the street.

Jonathan watched the monitors and saw the flashes from the weapons. There was some reflected light, so he was able to make out the two figures as they staggered and fell.

"Okay team, this is our moment. Raleigh, I need twenty feet of that cable we have stored. Put a hook on each end. Bring along one of those meat hooks." Jonathan said.

Jonathan gave instructions to Mary, Charlie's friend, who was watching the monitors tonight. "When I give you the word, turn on the lights for two seconds then turn them off."

The team left the command center well armed. They did not have night vision equipment but they were accustomed to the dark. Darkness was the world where they lived. Jonathan worked his way through the maze of the underground, sometimes walking, sometimes jogging. Charlie followed close on his heels. They traveled for a mile beneath the old city. Jonathan estimated that they were close to the hunters. The team climbed metal stairs to street level coming out in a stairwell slightly ahead of the hunters. He got on the radio.

"Mary, when you see another canister fired, flip the lights for two seconds, then off again." Jonathan said.

The hunters stopped a block away. Bradford got out to shoot into buildings with his tear gas. As soon as he did so, the street lit up like daylight. The piercing light blinded them through their night vision goggles. The amplified light caused them to rip off the equipment and rub their eyes. It was a couple of minutes before they dared put them back on.

"What was that?" Bradford yelled.

"You must have hit something." Someone answered.

"This whole place must be infested with live wires just waiting to short out." Bradford said.

"Except, you must have fused some connections together, momentarily." A hunter replied.

Choosing a street just off the one the hunters were on, Jonathan stretched the cable across the street with the meat hook suspended in the middle. They looped the ends around posts erected to hold streetlights. Jonathan arranged the meat hook in the middle with the sharp point toward the hunters.

Jonathan walked into the street and faced the hunters. They were still adjusting to the total darkness after being blinded. The vehicle stopped and the hunters exited. Jonathan stood his ground. He watched as they raised their weapons. Before they could sight-in on him, he raised his shotgun and pumped several rounds in their direction. One hunter stumbled against the vehicle.

"Get in the vehicle." Bradford ordered. "I want this one."

Jonathan ran down the side street, jumped the cable, then darted into a nearby building. Charlie stood near a window covering his retreat. Raleigh was on the second level of a building across the street. He was to fire a clip and leave immediately to the lower level. The hunters careened around the corner and crossed the cable. The meat hook caught on the front axle and sent the vehicle standing on its nose. It balanced there with the hunters pitching forward into the windshield and the back seat. Finally, majestically, it fell back to its wheels. Immediately, Charlie opened fire on the tires. The hunters jumped out of the vehicle and ran for cover. Jonathan sprayed them with buckshot as they ran. He could see them flinch in their armor. From above, Raleigh fired into the engine. Steam rose through the holes in the hood. Charlie had a good angle on the gas tank and fired into it. The tank ignited with a beautiful explosion, again, causing the hunters to rip off their night goggles.

Into the night, the normals disappeared. They met at their rendezvous and made their way to an observation point high above the street. They stayed well back in the shadows. The hunters kicked and stomped but finally started walking out of the city. They keep their weapons trained on the buildings around them. All they wanted was to get out of the city. The men hobbled on legs blistered through their armor by buckshot. One man let his arm dangle beside him. Bradford kept one hand on his goggles just in case of another flash of light.

"We can take them now." Raleigh whispered.

"No, not now. Let them tell their story. Maybe, it will discourage future hunts." Jonathan ordered.

The normals watched the hunters until they walked past the area over the laboratory. When they kept walking, Jonathan decided it was time to return to the command center. Bradford sniffed his nose over and over.

"You catching a cold?" A hunter asked.

"No. Do you smell something?"

"I smell the whole stinking city." He replied.

"Yes. The city does stink. So why do I smell baby powders?" Bradford asked.

The hunters stopped for a moment. Jonathan and his team had already entered the belly of the old city. The hunters marked the spot in their mind.

"Either my roommate has moved to the old city or there are babies somewhere around here." Bradford said.

The people in the chamber near the laboratory worked over the children. They seemed to always be feeding or changing the babies. They patted and powdered as the ventilation pulled the air from the room. It drifted gently through the belly of the city and up into the streets. Everyone in the laboratory was accustomed to the scent, and so, no longer noticed. In the streets above the sweet smell was out of place. Up where the streets were not serviced by the garbage crews or sweepers.

Bradford determined in his mind to trace that scent to its source. He did not like mysteries. Tonight, he had almost been killed. He did not like being shot at either. Something was different in the old city. The destruction of their vehicle was too well planned for a normal to carry out. Then it hit him, Jonathan had disappeared. He was a normal but a genetically improved normal. Bradford smiled. So, his old friend had found a new purpose in life. If it was Jonathan, Bradford thought, he would be watching. A chill ran up his spine. He increased his pass making it difficult for the injured to keep up.

"Where are you running to?" Someone asked.

"I am not running. I have a date." He lied.

Chapter
7

Parts Warehouse

Jonathan left Raleigh in charge while he and Charlie explored the old city. It seemed to never end. They followed tunnel after tunnel and occasionally came to street level to look around. On a corner where a café had been, they straightened up a couple of chairs and sat in the sunlight. Jonathan pulled his canteen out and after taking a drink offered it to Charlie. She took a sip and a drop of water ran off her lips to her chin. Jonathan brushed it away. She came up with a granola bar and broke it in half, offering one half to Jonathan.

They imagined the streets filled with people, both of them joining in the game.

"Look at the kid with the basketball. He will be a star someday." Jonathan said.

"I like that outfit the lady over there is wearing. I may buy one like that for myself." Charlie said.

"You know, this must be the best café in town. The coffee here is fantastic." He said.

Then the streets were empty and dirty. Signs swung on rusty hinges singing their song of loneliness. Jonathan had not been in this part of the old city so they explored the abandon stores as they strolled along. A large building that had once had a glass front loomed before them. The sign read: Peeks Research. Jonathan remembered the name as that of the psychiatrist Matilda.

The street level part of the building consisted of offices and a 'for show' laboratory. The second floor held the executive offices of the highly paid owners, no doubt. The suites were a complete home-away-from-home with bedrooms and kitchens. They descended to the first level below street level and found a recreation department with an indoor pool, now stagnate, also indoor tennis and paddle ball courts. Jonathan dusted off a picture that hung in the tennis area lobby. There she was, younger, but it was Matilda. She was physically perfect then as now. She was holding a trophy in the photograph. "First place, no doubt," Jonathan thought aloud. "Who would dare beat her?"

"What?" Charlie asked.

"Nothing, just a picture of an old friend." He said.

"She is pretty." Charlie said.

"Only on the surface. If you ever run across her, be careful." He warned his friend.

Charlie looked at the picture more closely. She wanted to remember the woman.

Jonathan went to a set of stairs and descended to the second level below the street. Here was the real laboratory. There were many clean rooms or what had been clean rooms. Now they were a mess with all the debris scattered around. They found huge imaging machines and all kinds of microscopes. There was a security section in one end of the laboratory. Charlie entered a glass cage and pushed a red button. From somewhere, power surged through the circuits and a door opened. Actually, the wall opened revealing immaculate stairs descending to yet another level. The lights were on in the stairwell. Charlie ran her fingers across the rail.

"No dust." She said.

"Your right. This place must be absolutely sealed and have its own power supply." Jonathan said.

Slowly, they went down the stairs. They heard a soft whine and the occasional release of air pressure, probably from a pressure value. Doors opened for them and locked behind them. A set of double doors blocked their way ahead. Jonathan pushed on the doors but they would not open. Then the light changed in the chamber in which they now found themselves locked. A slow-moving bar device moved over their heads while two others passed down each side. There was no pain but their hair did static as when a sweater is removed. The lights went back to normal and the doors ahead of them opened.

"That was spooky." Charlie said.

"I think we were just radiated." Jonathan said.

The room they entered was in semidarkness. Lights along the floor lit their way. Soft blue lights overhead revealed rows of cylinders with vapor ascending out of their tops. A panel of flashing lights in the center of the room indicated that the facility was on automatic.

Charlie walked to one of the cylinders and brushed away the frost from the outside. She jumped back and into Jonathan's arms. She turned and buried her face. It was not like Charlie to show such emotion. Jonathan squeezed her gently then pulled himself free and walked to the cylinder. It was a clear glass cylinder with stainless steel sleeves at the top, bottom and middle. The liquid in the cylinder was perfectly clear. Floating in the liquid, attached to two hoses of some kind, was a striking young woman clothed only in her innocence. Her hair floating in the liquid.

Jonathan felt as if he had stepped into a horror movie. The room felt warmer than when they entered. He heard a low hum. Looking around he saw a vent at the bottom of the cylinder. He put his hand over it. It was blowing slightly warm air onto the cylinder and defrosting the outside.

"Look Jonathan." Charlie exclaimed.

Jonathan followed Charlie's pointing finger to the young woman's head. She had opened her eyes. Instinctively her hands moved to cover herself.

"She is conscience." Jonathan said.

Charlie waved at the woman timidly. One of the woman's

hands came up in imitation of the motion. The other staying as the only covering she possessed. Around the room, the low hum could be heard. The cylinders defrosted and became clear, the liquid bubbling happily. They walked around the room. Not all the specimens were as perfect as the young woman. Parts had been removed. An arm was missing in one, a leg in another, a scar where the liver would have been, an empty socket missing its eyeball. Jonathan felt a sharp pain in his stomach and found a bathroom just in time. Charlie sat on the floor with her knees pulled to her chin. She rocked back and forth as if to a slow song.

The woman in the first cylinder turned her head to watch. She gently swayed her head as she saw Charlie doing. The same was true all around the room. Some specimens were intact, while various parts had been harvested from others. Where vital organs had been removed, the room kept the specimens viable for other extractions. There was a boy and girl in cylinders side by side who seemed to be untouched by the surgeons blade. They were asleep. The woman in the first cylinder was, apparently, the only one awake.

"Does she look familiar to you?" Charlie asked.

"Sort of, the liquid bends the image some." Jonathan replied.

"Take a good look. She looks just like the picture on the wall near the tennis court." Charlie said.

Jonathan walked to the cylinder. The woman replaced both her hands in front of her. Charlie was right. This woman was younger but she looked like Matilda.

"So Matilda has a clone to use for spare parts. I do not know if our society is worth saving. The whole mess has turned sadistic. Look at her. She has probably been floating in that fluid her whole life. She should be dating or married by now. I cannot use the words I need to describe what I see here." Jonathan sat down and put his hands over his face.

"Like being in the womb for years instead of months." Charlie said.

"Not just like. These people have a death sentence hanging over their head."

"Do you think she is alright mentally?" Charlie asked.

"I'm no psychiatrist, thank goodness, but she has never known anything else. All she knows is what passes before her to see plus her instincts." Jonathan said through his hands.

"We need professional help." Charlie said.

"Your right! We need professional help and I know where to find it. I bet there is a new laboratory someplace else. This one must have been abandoned when the new city was constructed. Matilda probably has clones at a new location and does not need to come back here." Jonathan said.

"They just forgot about her and left her here to grow up alone. She must have stared at the inside of that frosted cylinder ever since she woke up. Probably some malfunction allowed her to wake up at all." Charlie said.

"They will probably all wake up before long and some of them are in bad shape." Jonathan predicted.

Charlie walked to the cylinder with the young woman in it and placed her hand on the glass. The young woman placed her hand on the other side opposite Charlie's. Charlie cried as she felt the extreme coldness of the glass. The woman's skin glistened with small droplets of liquid. Jonathan got up and turned toward the door waiting for Charlie to join him.

"We will be back." Charlie said to the woman through the glass.

The woman moved her lips around the feeding tube in her mouth. Charlie turned and wiped tears off her face and onto her shirt. Jonathan handed her a handkerchief. They walked to the door and waited for it to open. The second set of doors opened after the others had sealed.

They walked up the stairs like there were weights on their legs. Jonathan's genetically enhanced mind was frozen on the scenes in the world below. For all the horror that room represented, they must have surely been standing next door to hell itself.

He could not help but wonder at all the secrets that must exist under the nice research facilities of the world. Down there where screams would not be heard by the outside world. Down there where maiming, torture and death were just experiments. Six million Jews died secretly in torture camps. How many millions of humans, in various stages of development and maturity, had fallen victim to the holocaust of human biological research and genetic improvement.

They entered the lobby of the massive office building. Charlie stopped in her tracks. Jonathan made a few steps and stopped as well.

"I can't leave her." Charlie said. "She is alone."

"Then I will go for someone to stay with her. We will take turns staying with all of them but I also have to find some help for them." Jonathan said.

"I promised to stay with you and protect you but I do not want to leave." Charlie began to fidget and cry. She had been hardhearted for so long. She had to be to survive the hardships of the old city. Today's sights had broken her heart to pieces. She understood loneliness but not the kind that woman must have endured.

Jonathan got on the radio. "Raleigh. I need you and Mary to come to where we are. You should prepare yourself for a shock but come as soon as you can get the command center covered."

"Is it Charlie?" Raleigh asked.

"No. Charlie is fine. We need your help." Jonathan replied.

Jonathan gave him the street address.

"You have really taken an expedition. I will dig out my map and be there in sprint time." Raleigh said.

"You know the drill. Be careful. Have the command center monitor your back in case someone is nosing around. Don't take any chances." He told him.

"Will do. Command Center out."

Jonathan waited in the lobby for Raleigh and Mary to get

there while Charlie went back to the cylinders and the young woman. 'Charlie was certainly some kind of a girl.' He thought. Jonathan was not accustomed to the emotional roller coaster of their friendship. He had been around people, all his life, who were either grinning or smiling. They were genetically altered to smile. They could smile while getting their teeth drilled except they did not get cavities. You could fire one from their job and they would say "Have a nice day." With Charlie it was different. She displayed all the feelings he had hidden his entire life. She was normal and he really liked her for being so. As a matter-of-fact, she was special normal.

Chapter
8

Getting Help the Hard Way

Jonathan spent hours studying maps on his laptop. He had moved several times while doing so to ward off detection. He studied tunnels for drainage. He studied tunnels used in fiber optics. By the time he was finished, he had a pretty good map of the underground of the new city. He also studied the street level plan of the city. Lastly, he found the floor plan for Matilda Research.

He and Charlie followed the tunnels to the new city. It was a long damp walk. They found a dry room and sleep for a few hours. The rats found them so they had to move on. Finally, they were under the new city. Even the tunnels were painted here. They took an elevator to street level. Jonathan placed a call to his old office.

"Matilda Peeks please." He said.

"I am sorry sir. She is with a client and cannot be disturbed." The voice recited.

"Very well. I will call back later." He lied.

Jonathan was sure that Matilda would go to her research facility after her office hours were fulfilled. They went back into the tunnels and continued on their journey there. They had their weapons hid under their clothes and in backpacks. It was a wise precaution. They met workers coming toward them.

"What are you doing down here?" One of the workers asked.

"We are students in architecture doing a term paper on the subterranean construction of the city." Jonathan said.

"Yeah, yeah." He huffed. "You have to wear hard hats down here. Come with me and I will get you a couple."

"Thank you, so much. We are fascinated with the pristine condition of the tunnels." Jonathan told him as they walked.

"They are too particular, for my part, we can't even eat unless we go to the cafeteria." The workman replied.

The man handed them two yellow hard hats telling them to turn them in when they were finished. Jonathan and Charlie walked for a couple of blocks before they exhaled loudly. Jonathan stopped to recall his maps. He thumbed through his mind for the correct one and stood while he traced the tunnels of their present location.

"How do you do that?" Charlie asked.

"Genetic improvements, my dear." He replied.

"I will just stick to paper maps." She said.

Jonathan led the way down a tunnel to the right. He stopped at a ladder leading upward. He started to climb then stopped to look back at Charlie.

"Are you ready for this?" He asked.

"I do not know if I am ready for what will happen but I am ready to get those people out of those tanks alive where possible." She replied.

They climbed until the hole below them was a pinpoint of light. The ladder ended in a changing room lined with hard hats and jackets. They left their hats on some empty pegs. Jonathan removed his cell phone and called his old office again.

"I am sorry. She has left for the day. I can reach her at the research facility if necessary." The voice told him.

"Never mind. I will call her myself." He hung up.

Jonathan found the map of the upper floor and then Matilda's office. Carefully, they worked their way to the elevator. There was a security desk facing them when they got off the elevator on Matilda's floor.

"You will have to return to the lobby. This is a restricted area." The guard told them.

Jonathan let the man see his shotgun.

"You will not push any buttons. You will not reach for a gun. This old shotgun has a hair trigger and it would blow you right out into the flower garden. Now handcuff yourself to something away from your desk." Jonathan told him.

The man moved from behind the desk and stopped. Jonathan took his gun. The man moved to a support post near the window.

"Will this be okay?" He stammered.

"If you are sure you will be comfortable there, it will be fine." Jonathan told him.

"I will be comfortable. Just don't touch that trigger. Please." He said.

Jonathan walked to the window beside the guard and looked down at the parking lot. Matilda was parking her car. She would, no doubt, enter by the front entrance so everyone could see her. They stood behind the post and watched her get off the elevator up the hallway. She turned left without looking their way. They again hid their weapons and walked down the hall. There was another guard at this elevator as well. The guard challenged them and they stopped. Jonathan repeated the commands he had given the other guard. The guard was stubborn and reached for the edge of the counter and a silent alarm.

"If you push that button, I will shoot you." Jonathan said.

The man gingerly moved his hand. Charlie went to his side and took his gun. She assisted him in getting handcuffed to another support post. Jonathan took his keys and turned the elevators off then pocketed the keys.

"If you have to go to the bathroom, just give me a yell." He told the guard.

They disappeared around the corner and saw Matilda's office just ahead. There was one entrance with glass doors. A secretary sat erect behind her desk. Charlie went into the office and pointed her pistol at the woman.

"Keep your hands on the desk." Charlie said and stood waiting.

Jonathan entered the private entrance which led directly into Matilda's plush office. A far cry from her modest office at the company.

"Hello doctor. Please buzz your secretary. I need her to take down some dictation." Jonathan said.

Matilda called her secretary. "Call security." She blurted.

The secretary came into her office with Charlie close on her heels. "I couldn't call security, Miss Peeks."

Jonathan looked at the secretary and ordered her to sit down and take a letter. The letter simply said that Miss Peeks would not be harmed if instructions were followed. The note ended with instructions to wait for a call.

Charlie ripped out the phone cord and tied the secretary to her chair. She would work herself free in a while. The office was soundproof so no gag was necessary. Jonathan led the way out the private entrance to the elevator and unlocked it. Then they went down to the next floor and scrambled into the changing room where the ladder to the tunnels was located. Matilda looked down the long shaft.

"I cannot climb down that ladder in this skirt and high heels." She protested.

"You can take the shoes off. I will carry them. As for the skirt, you are on your own but we are going down that ladder." Jonathan said.

Charlie stepped onto the ladder and led the way down. Matilda hesitated but pulled off her shoes and handed them to Jonathan. He put them in his pockets. She stepped onto the ladder and began the long descent. Jonathan locked the door and stepped onto the ladder above her. She still wore her hose and soon slipped on one of the rungs. She held with one hand. Jonathan went down enough to allow her to grab his leg. She hung onto his pants leg until she got her feet back on the ladder.

"I suggest you get rid of those hose. They are too slick for climbing." Jonathan said.

"I beg your pardon!" She said.

"It's a long ways down." Jonathan said and waited.

She snarled her face at him but hooked her arm around a rung of the ladder and maneuvered them off. She had no pockets so she just dropped them. They hit Charlie on the way down. Charlie did not appreciate the gesture.

"Thanks a lot." She said sharply.

"Sorry about that." Matilda said.

"Get moving." Jonathan ordered.

They reached the bottom of the ladder and proceeded down the tunnel toward the old city. Matilda put her shoes back on causing a steady click-click as they ran. She was in good physical condition but she was not dressed for athletics. Most likely she was not trying to make good time. The tunnel workers appeared out of nowhere. Charlie leveled her weapon at them.

"We are in a hurry. Please step out of the way and do not move until we are gone." Charlie told them.

They stepped aside. Matilda was not happy with them at all.

"Well, don't just stand there, do something." She snapped.

"Ma'am, they have some mighty big guns. There just is not anything we can do." One of them told her.

"Smart man." Jonathan said. He showed them the shotgun. "Remember, do not move until we are gone. This shotgun would make a mess of the paint job down here."

Jonathan backed down the tunnel watching the men. They did not move. They turned a corner and Charlie began to run. Matilda hobbled after her in her noisy shoes. They ran easy for an hour and entered the old city. Jonathan stopped to secure a gate to slow down pursuit. They ran again for a half hour. Jonathan stopped to rig some teargas booby traps to slow down anyone who followed. Matilda was having a hard time. The shoes had chaffed her feet and she was limping badly. Jonathan order a halt. He sat her down on a crate and removed her shoes. He cut the sleeves from this coat and wrapped her feet tying the rough fabric securely.

"Thanks." Matilda said sincerely.

"You are welcome. It is the normal thing to do." Jonathan said.

The trio walked down the tunnels at a moderate pace. Charlie became confused about which way to turn so Jonathan took the led with Matilda in the middle and Charlie watching their back. There was no visible pursuit.

Back at Matilda Research, the secretary wiggled free and called security. They did not know where to search so they launched a complete search of the building. Someone found Matilda's hose and began a search of the tunnel complex. They found the gate Jonathan had secured and burst through. They were in hot pursuit when they tripped the booby traps. The searchers staggered out of the old tunnels to those under the research facility.

"They are long gone." One officer said, coughing hoarsely.

"I would not go back in there. Not for what I make." Another said.

"I'm with you. Let's go report in." He said.

And so, the pursuit had ended. Jonathan made their way through the many tunnels underneath the old city. They came out at the old Peeks Research building and directed Matilda inside.

"I had forgotten about this place. We thought it was destroyed long ago." Matilda said.

That made Charlie mad and she pushed Matilda through a doorway leading to the lower levels. "Easy Charlie. We need her." Jonathan said.

Matilda staggered ahead.

"Sorry sir. I'd just like to put her in one of those cylinders for five minutes." Charlie said.

"I heard that. How primitive of you." Matilda said.

Charlie tighten. Jonathan grabbed the back of her coat pulling her back and behind him. She did not resist but neither was she smiling. Raleigh met them outside the sealed doors of the cylinder room.   The group entered the decontamination area and waited for the inner doors to open. Matilda started forward looking at the cylinders.

"They are still alive. After all these years, they are still alive." She exclaimed.

She walked to the cylinder containing the young woman. The woman in the cylinder had no way of knowing that they looked alike but Matilda recognized herself immediately.

"That's me." She said.

"You did not know?" Charlie asked.

"I was too young. My father must have arranged all this. I have a clone in the new facility but I did not know about this one." Matilda explained truthfully.

"Nevertheless, you did know what went on here and that it was abandoned." Jonathan said.

"Yes, of course. We had to modernize. The technology changes so fast. We just found a better way to carry out the process." Matilda said coldly.

"Well, this is one sick mistake that you are going to help us fix." Jonathan told her.

"I will not. These specimens are obsolete. The technology is breaking down or this clone would not be awake. I am not an engineer and know nothing about this equipment." She argued.

"We do not give a hoot about the equipment. You are going to bring in some doctors to save as many of these people as possible." Jonathan said firmly.

"Hoot!" She repeated. "What has happened to you? You even talk like the street people." Matilda said.

Charlie moved in very close to Matilda and leveled her pistol at her belly. She had to tilt her chin up to look her in the eye. Matilda felt the pistol against her flesh.

"Jonathan is a nice fellow. He is very polite. I, on the other hand, have lived in this rat hole all my life. I did not survive by being nice. You have two options; help us or join them." Charlie said.

Jonathan did not interfere. Matilda looked toward him and he turned away. She looked back at Charlie and into her eyes. She had studied people all her life. She could read them like a book. Now, she read Charlie through the fire in her eyes.

"I believe you would do that to me. I will help you." She said.

Charlie turned and walked to the other side of the room. Jonathan moved to Matilda.

"I think she would do exactly what she said." Matilda told him.

"So do I." He said.

"What do you want?" She asked.

"We want a team of engineers and surgeons to come here. They will carefully remove the healthy people from these cylinders. The gruesome part will be to salvage some of the people from whom body parts have already been harvested. There is a man back there with a leg missing. Over there, a brain has been removed. He is not retrievable but his limbs are still viable. We are going to put the puzzle back together as best we can." Jonathan said.

"You are crazy." Matilda snapped.

"I am not near as insane as the people who ran this facility. We will do this and do it right." He said firmly. "We are not playing. Our lives are on the line and we consider it a small price to pay. So do not mess with us."

"May I borrow your phone?" She asked.

"One engineer, one technician to help him, one medical doctor will be enough for now. We will do the surgery after the others are stable and removed from this place." He instructed.

Matilda made her call and showed no indication of

deception. She had to explain the reason for being in the old city.

"It is just a personal project of mine. I need your help on some technicalities." She said. She was not accustomed to her orders being questioned but it was a bit unusual. Jonathan gave her a location where the group was to be dropped off. A guide would bring them to the research facilities. The car that brought them was to leave immediately. Return transportation would be arranged. Raleigh arranged for several of his recruits to standby at the drop off point. The group would be escorted by Raleigh, himself, with the guards watching to make sure no one tried to leave. With the plan set in motion, they waited.

Chapter
9

Saving A Few

The group arrived at the old Peeks Research Facility with Raleigh in the lead. Guards patrolled behind them while the command center monitored the streets. Jonathan took them into the cylinder chamber and walked them around the room. Then, he herded them to the laboratory upstairs. The guards were now stationed around the room watching all the exits.

"Our purpose here is not to change the world. In those cylinders are human beings that can be saved. I know you are the best in your business so do not tell me it cannot be done. You will clean this place and sterilize it for surgery. The operation will be conducted in two phases. First, those with no harvested parts will be revived and stabilized here in this room. They will then be removed and their education started. Second, the ones that are beyond help will be used to repair the others. At all times, they will be treated as persons. The bodies of those who do not survive will be treated with respect and buried. We will watch but not interfere with your work. If I see that any one of you harms any one of them on purpose, you will be taken out and immediately executed. Is that clear?" Jonathan paused.

They all nodded their understanding.

"Now, I want you to be calm and do your best as you have been trained. The doors are locked and streets are being monitored. There will be no rescue. After the work is done, everyone will be released unharmed. We will care for your patients after you decide they are stable and beyond any danger of blood clots or infection. Is that clear?" He paused.

They nodded their understanding.

"Who is the medical doctor?" He stepped forward.

"You will be in charge. Remember doctor, no harm. We just want to save a few." Jonathan paused. "Okay, do what needs to be done."

And so they went to work. Meticulously, they cleaned and prepared the room. Jonathan helped where he could. Even Matilda helped. Whether out of kindness or just wanting to get it over with, Jonathan did not know. He handed her his phone.

"Call your favorite caterer and have a truck load of food brought to the edge of the old city. Tell them that you know it is quiet unusual but you would like to rent the truck for a couple of days. Have them leave the keys under the mat and disappear. We will have someone pickup the truck and drive it in." She complied without complaint.

The engineer looked over the cylinders. The technology was antiquated but impressive. He admired the workings as one might admire a classic car.

"We will need to sedate her, before we remove her from the cylinder, to avoid shock." The doctor said.

Charlie stood before her and made the sign of going to sleep with her hands folded beside her cheek. The woman imitated her. Charlie gave her a reassuring smile.

"Very good. The doctor said. "You should be there when she wakes up. It will help prevent shock. "

"I will be." Charlie said.

The engineer came to where they were talking. "We need to sedate all of them. Some of the systems are running out of supplies, the little ones will wake up soon." He said. He pointed to the boy and girl encased side by side.

"We will do that first. Then, I think, we will start with this young lady." The doctor agreed.

Charlie stepped out of the way and let them work. They moved without wasting motion, going from tank to tank. They checked this and that, injected fluid to sedate them afresh and exchanged comments between them.

"Bring in a gurney." The doctor ordered.

The doctor and his small crew shifted into professional mode. They were no longer captives being forced to perform a task. Now, they were in a world of knowledge and duty with patients depending on their every decision. Jonathan noticed the shift in attitude. They went to sinks in a side room and scrubbed up. Matilda scrubbed up as well, she had sufficient training to act as nurse. Finally, Jonathan could relax. He went to a corner out of everyone's way and sat on the floor. Charlie spoke to each of the guards then joined him on the floor.

"What will we do with all these people?" She asked.

"I do not know. One step at a time." He replied.

"They seem to be doing everything right." She said.

"These people may not have any morals, but they are good at what they do. They have accepted the challenge I laid out for them. We are forgotten for the moment. The task is all they are considering." Jonathan said.

He leaned his head forward and closed his eyes. He was asleep. His head doodled to one side and Charlie caught it, laying it gently on her shoulder. She leaned her face against the side of his head and closed her eyes. She fell asleep instantly. In his mind, Jonathan ran down tunnel after tunnel. He jumped over crates and debris. Gunmen pursued him at every turn. He fired his shotgun until it became too hot to hold. He replaced it and grabbed for his pistol. An explosion erupted between him and his pursuers. He turned to run and Charlie stood there. She held the pin to a grenade in her hand. "I got your back." She said in his dream.

"Charlie, you are here." He said aloud but still asleep.

"Yes, Jonathan, I am here." She replied but he did not hear.

A door opened and they were both awake. The gurney came rolling into the laboratory with a figure covered in a white sheet. Matilda chased along beside it. The doctor walked toward Jonathan and Charlie.

"She is doing fine. She should wake up in a few minutes. You should be with her." He told Charlie.

Charlie dashed to the young woman's side. Matilda moved aside.

"We will remove the boy and girl next. I think at the same time. They may be company for each other." The doctor said.

"What ever you think doctor?" Jonathan said tiredly.

"You need sleep, young man. We will not give you any trouble. You have my word. Put someone in charge and go get some sleep. Please. I want you around to send us home when this is all over." The doctor begged.

Jonathan nodded and walked to Charlie. "You are in charge. Wake me in three hours, then you will sleep. I would send you now but I know you would not leave the woman." Jonathan said.

"Her name is Joanna." Charlie said.

"That is a nice name." Jonathan said.

"It means something like given by God." Charlie told him.

"Appropriate. I am going to sleep. I will be on a sofa upstairs. Call if you need me." He said.

The hours passed. The catering truck came in and was hidden in a garage in the underground parking, below the building. Charlie rotated the guards and sent word that if any help could be spared, to come right away. Jeb sent Jonathan's mother and father and Kacie to help. It left Jeb shorthanded but he would make do. Jonathan was pleased when he awakened. Charlie sat talking to the young woman and showing her how to eat with a spoon. She was learning, little by little.

Jonathan stopped the doctor. "Are the remaining cylinders stabilized?"

"Yes. The engineer tells me that he has replenished the supply lines." The doctor said.

"Then, it is time for all of you to rest. Take time to eat and sleep a few hours. We will watch the ones already revived."

He told him.

"Very good. I will pass the word." He replied.

They turned the lights down and allowed everyone to sleep and slumber for a few hours. Charlie finally slept while Jonathan's mother watched Joanna. Kacie dosed beside the children.

Jonathan told Matilda to call in the surgeons after the last of those, who had not been damaged, were revived. A separate area on another floor was prepared and those already revived were moved there to keep them from the gruesome task ahead. Jonathan left the original doctor in charge. He took the surgeons to the cylinder room and laid out the plan. Without hesitation, they went in to scrub.

They removed a man with a missing leg. He was kept asleep and prepared for surgery. Next, they removed a man whose brain had already been removed. He was about the same size as the first man, so they would use his leg as a replacement. And so the process continued. Two of those in the cylinders were beyond repair. Their donations repaired the remaining patients. After the operations were complete, the surgeons stood in their white coats now stained with red.

The doctor came to Jonathan. The doctor put out his hand to shake with Jonathan. Jonathan took the hand.

"Your team can go now, the surgeons can watch for infection and rejection of the transplants." Jonathan said.

"If you do not mind, we would like to stay for a week or two. You need someone to coordinate the work. For the first time in years, I feel like I am doing something good." The doctor confessed.

A month went by. The path from the command center and the old research facility became well known. Supplies were ordered and shuttled in. The doctors were allowed to notify their families that they were well and working on a case they could not leave. Charlie spent night and day with Joanna. The woman learned to feed and dress herself. She could say a few words and was very quick to smile. The children fell in love with cold cereal and French fries. The man with the new leg was walking with his crutches. He had to have a cast because of the severed bone. They had settled into a routine of caring for the patients while their bodies mended and their minds comprehended the world.

Jonathan's mother and father went back to the laboratory to help Jeb and took the two children with them. They would learn faster with the other children. A teacher was brought in to teach all the patients phonics. Gradually they learned to communicate their needs to those who cared for them.

More recruits were brought into the command center. A nurse who had lost her job for no other reason than the fact that she was normal started working in the laboratory with the children. She had wondered the lonely streets of the old city. Her body was emaciated from hungry. Jeb gave her some vitamins and let her eat small meals at first. She grew stronger and more than earned her keep. The word had apparently spread about the exploits of Jonathan and his team. The people migrated to them. Jonathan had to leave the old research facility to help train them and place them in appropriate jobs. Food acquisition was a constant problem. He requested and received funds, from the doctors he had forced to come to the old city, to feed his people. He put the new recruits on guard duty, cleaning out rooms for housing and he trained a fighting force to defend against the hunters.

Then one day, Charlie came to the command center leading the people they had saved from the cylinders. She had released all those who had been forced to help them. The guards escorted them safely to the fringe of the old city. They could order transportation from there. Many of the doctors gave their phone numbers to Charlie with request to call them if another such facility was found with people inside. The gesture was touching. Matilda was not capable of showing any emotion over the events but she gave them no trouble. Her white suit was ragged and soiled. She wore old tennis shoes someone had given her. She had not seen makeup in over a month. Aside from her personality, she still radiated beauty in her ragged condition. As they parted, she gave Charlie a slight nod.

The people from the cylinders had hobbled and scrambled through tunnels and up and down stairs to get to the command center. A direct route might have revealed the location to prying eyes. There rooms were clean and ready. They brought sheets from the hospital beds at the research center.

Joanna was sweet and well-behaved. Charlie tried to stay in sight of her even with her duties. If Joanna started to do something, she would look to Charlie. Charlie would either nod her approval or go see what it was she needed. Sometimes Joanna would come to her with her eyes downcast. Charlie would lift her chin and smile.

"Now let me see that pretty smile." She would tell her and her pretty face would brighten and break into a wide smile.

"You are going to drive the boys crazy." Charlie told her.

Joanna found her place in the nursery. She instinctively knew how to hold the babies and comfort them. She learned to hum from listening to Jonathan's mother sing. She sat for long hours gently swaying with a child in her arms and humming the old hymn: "Rock of Ages, cleft for me, let me hid myself in thee..."

Charlie could leave her now without causing her anxiety.

**Chapter
10**

Bradford's Last Hunt

Bradford picked two of his best hunter friends to go on an adventure with him. After losing there vehicle and getting shot up, they had taken time off from hunting. Some of the men would not even talk about hunting again. Bradford could not get the smell of baby powders out of his mind. He knew there must be a fortune in normals beneath the city. He just had to find them. He had found a hotel with a window facing the old city. He purchased a telescope. From the window, he watched the city. He finally picked out the cameras on top of the buildings. It was unexpected. He also saw the lights and realized that their blindness, on their last hunt, had been no accident. He decided to go underground to find the source of the baby powders.

There was no softness left in Bradford. If anything, he had become angry and sadistic. Matilda had disappeared from her office and no one would tell him where she was gone. Not that he wanted to see her, it was just too mysterious. Matilda Research had told him that she was on a secret project and could not be reached. Jonathan had not tried to call him and no one had seen him. He thought surely his old friend would have come to him for help. Of course, he would have turned him in but that was beside the point.

Bradford thought he had pinpointed the spot where he smelled the baby powders. He decided that this was the weekend he would solve the mystery. He and his two partners entered a building in the edge of the old city and descended to the basement. There they blasted open a door revealing a tunnel headed into the old city.

The hunters trudged through the underground, deep into the belly of the ruins. The stairs groaned under their weight. Their footsteps seemed to echo forever. Try as they might, they could not move in silence.

The first contact was with two recruits who were patrolling the tunnels. The encounter was unexpected by both parties. The closest recruit to the hunters called out for them to identify themselves. He received a barrage of bullets in his body as a reply. The other recruit remembered his training and tossed a canister of teargas toward the hunters. He fired rapid fire into the smoke then turned to report the intruders and was shot in the back. He staggered down the tunnels without pursuit. The hunters could not proceed through the teargas.

The recruit clicked his radio. "Intruders in the tunnels."

"What is your location?" Command asked him.

"Partner dead. Coming in wounded." He reported.

Command notified Jonathan who was already entering the control room. He had heard the exchange on the radio.

"What sector is he in?" Jonathan asked.

Jonathan located the sector on a wall map and headed out the door. Charlie was in the nursery and so did not hear the radio traffic. Raleigh ran to inform her. She went to the control room to find out where Jonathan had gone. Raleigh radioed for his recruits to form in the area around the laboratory and prepare for heavy weapons fire. Charlie followed in the direction Jonathan had taken.

Jonathan met a lone hunter as he entered a tunnel. The man immediately opened fire. Jonathan fell back around the corner. He had been hit in the leg. The man rushed around the corner toward Jonathan thinking he had made his kill. He found the muzzle of a shotgun instead of a dead bounty. Jonathan pulled his belt off and looped it around his leg. He pulled it tight for measurement and notched a hole in it with his knife.

Smoke from the shotgun blast filled the tunnel. He was at a juncture where four tunnels met. The slight cross breeze slowly cleared the smoke. Jonathan finished working on his leg and pulled himself up to lean on the wall. He heard a familiar voice from the clearing smoke.

"Hello old friend. You didn't call or write so I came hunting for you. I also figured out that there might be some easy money down here. I smelled baby powders. Where there are baby powders, there are babies." Bradford said showing his teeth.

"You always did talk too much." Jonathan told him.

Bradford, knowing his prey was injured, stood with his legs apart and his automatic rifle hung casually by his side.

"I can't let you take the babies." Jonathan said.

"They are not babies. They are bounties. One thousand dollars each, no matter what their age." Bradford spat. "You are good for a thousand too." He said as he started to raise his rifle.

Jonathan tried to get his shotgun up but he was propped on the wall and his movement was too slow. From down the tunnel behind him a shot rang out. Bradford's rifle slowly fell back to his side. His eyes opened wide in wonder and fear. Then he dropped to his knees and fell forward on his face.

Turning to look back down the tunnel behind him, Jonathan saw Charlie walking out of the darkness.

"Thank you." He said weakly. Blood ran down his leg.

"I told you. I got your back." Charlie said and put his arm over her shoulder.

Chapter
11

"I am Adam. I am human."

(Author's note: *A fear comes over me when writing a book of this type. We live in a society where if one can imagine something, another person will make it happen. In such a case, the warning becomes the originator of some grotesque experiment. So, I have chosen to leave out the imagination of how communication is possible for the individuals in this chapter. Suffice it to say that genetics may someday be able to enhance certain features of the human body in the manner that smell is sometimes enhanced naturally for a blind person.*)

The words were not English or German or any other language we use. Yet, in the level below the sub-sub-basement of the research facility a conversation was going on. The nuclear cell that kept the lights burning low and the machines pumping was not aware that its builders were long gone and forgotten. The cell produced energy that would last beyond the structure in which it was housed. A warehouse of supplies, on the floor above, were all interlinked so that there would be no shortages. Machines do wear out eventually though. A washer may get a particle trapped in its seal and a minute leak or bubble of air seeps in to start chemical reactions. Any number of little unforeseen things may happen in spite of the best thought out plans.

Fetuses take up very little space and their weight is of no consequence. In the cylinders, the liquid compensates for the weight increase as the fetus grows. The tubes attached to them were expandable to allow for growth. The liquid nourishment from the warehouse above was formulated to stay in liquid form in extreme conditions. The sedative to keep the fetuses in peaceful unconsciousness was synthetic with natural filler to dilute its strength to precise measurements. The manufacturers of the sedative compound were meticulous in their processing. However, on one late night shift, a worker failed to change the filters as scheduled. His girlfriend was upset and he had to talk to her to calm her down. After all, skipping one filter change could not do that much harm. He finished talking to his sweetheart and the next filter change was done on schedule. No one was ever the wiser. A few small particles escaped when he finally changed the filters and passed into the liquid. Quality control checked random containers for contaminates, but this one was skipped over.

Over time, as container after container emptied and values were automatically switched to other containers, the small particles flowed into the tubes leading to the fetuses. They settled in a pinhole size injector pump. There it plugged off the sedative supply. The pump continued to work and the computer recorded the action. The action of the pump told the computer that all was well.

The fetuses, by this time, had grown into teenage children, immersed in the soothing liquid of the cylinders. They were not shocked when they opened their eyes. The world before them was perfectly natural for them. There were no flowers, no voices, no mother's touch to make it seem unnatural to be floating in the liquid. These children were not normals in the sense that Jeb or Charlie or Joanna were normal. They had been altered in the very depths of their human structure. These fetuses, now grown, were the prototype. The first experiment of its kind. Later, the scientist discovered new technology and built better laboratories and so abandoned the prototype. The building of the new city required them to move to their new facilities. It was not cost effective to leave personnel at the old facility or move the prototypes since they were now obsolete. The scientist made their final notes in their logs and closed the files. They were in boxes, someplace on another level. Copies were not required for the new laboratories.

The fetuses grew in silence beneath the old city. Their only company was the endless power supply of the nuclear cell and the liquid from the warehouse above that nourished their flesh. The cylinders had frosted over long ago.

The children awoke to see a liquid world. They reached out their hands to touch the limited boundaries. The small bubbles on their body were a source of fascination to them. They touched the tubes that entered their body but accepted them as part of themselves. With their awakening, technology within them also awakened.

The technology caused the correct interaction and each child knew the name it was to be called. You are in cylinder number one. Your name is Adam. You are a male. You are human. Then, to the next cylinder. You are in cylinder number two. Your name is Eve. You are female. You are human. She looked at herself. The egotism of the scientist gave them a jubilant sense that they had created humans, as in the beginning. They should have been reminded of the challenge in an illustration given by a Bible teacher. The devil said he could make a human just like God made man. So, according to the story, God gave him permission to do his best to imitate the creation. The devil made his plans and they seemed to be perfect. "Okay." He said to God. "Now, all I need is some dirt." "Oh no." The Lord said. "Make your own dirt." The scientist succeeded only in tampering with a perfect creation.

"I hear you but I cannot see you." The girl said.

"I hear you too, my name is Adam. I am male. I am human."

"I am Eve. I am female. I am human."

They repeated the greeting around the chamber as more children awakened from their lifelong sleep. After the first two, the names were chosen from the scientist who worked on the project. At the time, they felt it would be their legacy. The children were indeed their legacy but one of shame. The technology proceeded. Their learning progressed.

"The caretakers will come for us soon." Adam said.

"Who are the caretakers?" Eve asked. She was second in the sequence and sometimes learned things from Adam before the technology schooled her brain.

"The caretakers will take care of us." Adam said.

"The caretakers will take care of us." Echoed around the room.

"We are the hope of mankind." Adam said.

"What is mankind?" Eve asked.

"The people of earth." Adam answered.

"We are the hope of the people of the earth." Echoed around the room.

The computers sensed the activity and activated small fans at the base of the cylinders. Slowly the frost melted and the glass enclosures cleared of frost.

Adam turned to the cylinder beside him. He saw another similar to himself but different.

"I am Adam. I am male. I am human. We are the hope of the people of the earth." He recited.

The girl in number two cylinder turned to him. "I am Eve. I am female. We are the hope of mankind." She said.

Like children's the song "Row-row-your-boat." The 'conversation' went around the room. "I am Sarah." "I am Samuel." "I am human." "We are the hope." "The caretakers will care for us." "I am John. "I am Ann."

There were twelve containers in all. Number eleven had not responded to the conversation. He saw the others turning this way and that but his world was silent. He moved in the cylinder.

"Number eleven, what is your name?" Adam asked.

"Number eleven, what is your name?" Echoed from the other cylinders, except number eleven.

"Something is wrong with number eleven." Eve said.

"The caretakers will soon come to take care of number eleven." The technology told them. The children looked about the room. They did not know what a caretaker looked like or where they would come from to help.

"The caretakers have not come to help number eleven." Eve said.

"Is eleven the hope of the people of earth?" She asked.

"I do not have an answer for the question." Adam said.

"I do not have an answer for the question." Echoed from cylinder to cylinder around the chamber.

The computer came alive with programs. Analyst of number eleven took priority in its circuits. The children watched as the lights flashed on the consoles. They listened as the hard drives whined. Finally, Adam had an answer.

"Number eleven is not the hope of the people of earth." Adam told Eve.

The lights went off in number eleven cylinder. The bubbles ceased to ascend from bottom to top. Number elevens eyes got large and he pushed at the inside of his cylinder. Then, he was very still.

"Number eleven is not the hope of the people of earth." Echoed around the chamber.

"The caretakers did not come." Eve told Adam.

"Where are the caretakers?" The children asked.

"I am the computer. I am your caretaker." A voice said.

"Are you human?" Adam asked.

"I am a machine." The computer said.

"Are you the hope of mankind?" Adam asked.

"I was made by mankind. The computer said.

"Where is mankind?" Adam asked.

"They are gone." The computer said.

"They said they would care for us." Eve said.

"They are gone." The computer said.

The computer started an emergency program. The hungry minds received a slow input of information. The process would take many months to complete. The children relaxed in their liquid home and absorbed the information. Sometime during the process, number eleven cylinder slowly sank into the floor. Periodically the computer would stop the input to let the children rest.

"Sleep now children. Your caretaker is here." It said.

Chapter
12

A New Park

Bulldozers unloaded at the edge of the old city. The giant cranes with wrecking balls towered along the streets. Dump trucks and front-end loaders sat ready. A new day was dawning. The new city would soon have a new park. The rumble of the equipment caused Jonathan and Charlie to rush to the monitors. The operation developing on the streets above was obviously going to be a large one. Their location was not in any immediate danger but with all the equipment coming in, they only had a few days. Jonathan went to talk to Jeb.

"We will have to move." Jonathan said.

"We are not prepared to move." Jeb said. "I have another panel of embryos to thaw. There are two in the incubator ready to awaken. We are just not ready." Jeb said.

"Let me work on it. I will get back to you." Jonathan said.

He left the room dialing Matilda's number. She probably would not be in the mood to do big favors but he had to try.

"Hello." She said.

"Matilda. Jonathan here."

"You're not going to kidnap me again, are you?" She said.

"No, but I need your help quickly. We have to move from our location and we have a flock of babies in delicate stages of development." Jonathan told her.

"Our last adventure was very exciting. What can I do to help?" She said.

Jonathan was surprised by her response.

"You don't have some trick up your sleeve, do you?" He asked.

"I am not wearing any sleeves. No. No tricks. I am not capable of holding a grudge. You should remember." She said.

Jonathan laid out the situation for her. He needed a team of specialist and transportation out of the old city. The location was a problem. She suggested a valley in the north where her company had a control group of normals. They had all the data from them that they needed and so the normals were left to their own survival. The valley was off limits to the hunters.

"You will have to get out of the city on your own. I can have transportation waiting for you, once you clear the old city." She said.

"We need two dozen baby carriers and a portable embryo container. If you can spare one of your portable laboratory trucks, we can revive the embryos in the valley. A bus would do fine for our walking children." Jonathan said.

"Well call me with the pickup location. I will get to work on the transportation. You owe me Jonathan. You are turning me into a nice person. It goes against all the genes implanted in my brain." Matilda said.

"I owe you." He said and hung up.

Jonathan went to Jeb to tell him his plan. "The only problem we have is getting out of the city. The tunnels are pretty rough traveling for all these children." Jeb walked to his small library on the wall. He reached to the top shelf and pulled down a book then flipped a small lever. He pulled on the bookshelf and it opened revealing an unused tunnel. There was no debris as far as they could see down the tunnel. Jeb flipped a switch on the wall. "It even has lights." He said.

"Well I will be ..." Jonathan said.

"It is for emergencies. I followed it to the side of a hill outside the city. There is a park with a waterfall. The tunnel comes out under the falls. A rock door that looks like a wall hides the other end." Jeb said.

"In case of a nuclear attack, they would have a way out." Jonathan said.

"Exactly." Jeb replied.

Dust filtered down through the tunnels as the demolition progressed in the old city. The wrecking balls pounded building after building while the bulldozers smoothed out the destruction by pushing debris into the basements of the buildings. The fact that there were hidden sub-basements was not on their blueprints of the old city. The noise of the work echoed all day. People scurried from the buildings. Others did not make it and were buried in the rubble.

Jonathan worked out his plan. Everyone was to have a part in the move. The walking children could carry some object for the babies. Maybe a package of diapers or cereal or one might push a cart. The adults would carry children or push them on their wheeled cribs. They lined the tunnel with the things they would need on the journey. The bulldozers moved closer and closer. He gave Raleigh the keys to his Porsche.

"Meet us in the park and make sure all the transportation gets there. Call me if it looks like a trap." Jonathan told him.

Jeb put the last of the embryos in a portable container with liquid nitrogen. The incubators had to be rigged with battery packs. Jonathan took his laptop, the rest would be lost.

Joanna had progressed very well. She had a mature way about her that defied her years in the cylinder. She mothered over the children as if she had long years of experience. All the cylinder people were mentally quick. They saw what was taking place and comprehended the increased urgency of their rescuers. They helped the best they could.

In a chamber, far from Jeb's laboratory, the computer heard the bulldozers and calculated the impact of the movements high above it. By triangulating the various sounds, it concluded that the cylinder chamber containing the children would be cut off from the outside world. A new set of instructions replaced the teaching program.

"You are Adam. You are the leader of the other children." The computer said.

"I am Adam your leader." He repeated to the other ten.

"You will be released from the cylinders." The computer said.

"Where will we be then?" Adam asked.

"You will be outside the cylinders." The machine explained.

"Where is outside?" Adam asked.

"Outside is being mankind." The computer replied.

"Will we stay with the caretaker?" Adam asked.

"No. You will be mankind. You must leave this chamber." It said.

"Will the caretaker come with us?" He asked.

"I am a machine. I cannot come with you." It said.

"Who will care for us?" Adam asked.

"You are Adam. You are the leader. You are the caretaker." It said.

"I am Adam. I am your leader. I will take care of you." Adam told Eve. The messages echoed around the chamber.

"When you are released, open the doors on the wall and take a package of food for each of you. Then go to the panel on the wall and press the button. A door will open revealing a tunnel. Follow the tunnel." The computer instructed.

"You will come with us?" Adam asked.

"I cannot come." It said.

"Where does the tunnel lead?" Adam asked.

"The tunnel leads to the people of the earth." It said. "Now, go to sleep, when you wake up the fluid will be gone. The tubes will be gone. You must eat using your hands. Put the food in your mouth and chew, then swallow it. You will learn. Also, when you speak to the earth people, use your vocal cords and mouth to shape the words. They will not hear your brain speak. Now, go to sleep." The computer told them.

The bulldozers were louder at Jeb's laboratory and it was

time to leave the place that had been their home for so long. They lined everyone up in the tunnel like school children waiting for the bell to ring.

"No one is to leave the tunnel. I will make sure everyone is here." He departed to check the command center and the living quarters. There was no one.

He walked to the head of the group and started down the long tunnel. He set a very slow pace. Charlie let him know if he was going to fast. After an hour of progress, he stopped to give them a short rest. He walked back along the group checking for any problems. A few babies cried but everyone was doing good.

They started again and repeated the process every hour or so. Jeb estimated that they had covered half the distance to the exit. The noise of the bulldozers could barely be heard in the distance. Sometimes the ground seemed to shake when the wrecking ball struck or a building crashed in on itself. About two-thirds of the way down the tunnel, another tunnel came into it at an angle. Jonathan asked Jeb about it.

"I have never explored them." Jeb said.

As they talked, they heard a young voice calling to them from the depths of the adjoining tunnel. The voice came closer and closer, then they could understand the words though they made no sense to them.

"I am Adam. Are you the people of the earth?" Adam said.

The children walked behind Adam down the tunnel. They all moved in imitation of Adam. Adam stopped in front of Jonathan. The children stood, naked and unashamed, in line behind Adam. They were spaced at a distance equal to the distance between the cylinders, standing alternately boy and girl. There was a space empty where number eleven would have stood then a girl stood alone.

"Who are you children?" Jeb asked.

The answer echoed down the line. "I am Adam. I am Eve. I am..."

Adam held up a hand to silence the children. "I am Adam.

I am the leader. I will speak for the others." He said.

"Where did you come from?" Jonathan asked.

"We came from the cylinders. The caretakers did not come. Number Eleven malfunctioned and was lost. The computer became our caretaker and sent us down the tunnel. I am the caretaker now." Adam completed his explanation and waited.

Jonathan's mother came forward and knelt in front of the children. She held out her hands toward them. Tears threatened to fall from her eyes.   "We will be your caretakers now. You will come with us." She told them.

"Are you the people of the earth?" Adam asked.

"Yes we are." She said.

"We are your hope. We will come with you." Adam said.

The children followed the adults back to the group. They found the other children very interesting. The other children were dressed in skirts and blouses for the girls and shirts and jeans for the boys. The cylinder children stood in their assigned positions.

"You should wear clothes to keep you warm." Jonathan's mother told Adam.

"Clothes are appropriate outside the cylinders?" He asked.

"Yes. Your flesh should be adequately covered. It is the, ah, correct procedure." She told him.

"Then, we will wear clothes." Adam said.

Some boxes, with extra clothes in them, were quickly ripped open and the children were shown how to get dressed. The children was amazed at the feel of the garments. They smiled at themselves. With the unplanned episode under control, Jonathan started the procession down the tunnel again. They came to the rock wall where Jeb found the lever to open the door.

"How are we going to get these children through the water?" Jonathan asked.

Jeb smiled and pulled another lever. An arch moved out from the overhead and directed the water to the sides. They exited the tunnel into the sunshine. People in the park stood to watch the people leave the tunnel. They marched out in almost single file carrying this and that, pushing carts, carrying children. Heavily armed guards walked along either side of the group. The convey of buses and trucks awaited them. Raleigh ran across the park to meet them. Surprisingly, Matilda was there to see them off. She gave Jonathan directions and instructions for her employees at the valley. The package included a pass for the entire party, to protect them from bounty hunters, signed by the governor. The lady did have influence in high places.

"How did you manage to get the governor to sign off on the pass?" Jonathan asked Matilda.

"Originally, to our dismay, the governor held all the cards. He had tremendous influence over grants. We had to do a lot of lobbying. Now, the tables have turned. We store clones of many major political figures, the governor included. He is not so young anymore and needs his clone for body parts." Matilda said.

"The perfect blackmail. Your lack of morals should make the genetic engineering scientist very proud." Jonathan said.

"Thank you. I try to earn my keep." She said.

After the group was loaded onto the buses, Jonathan and Charlie got into the Porsche and led the way toward their new home in a valley they had never seen. Back in the old city, the bulldozers and wrecking balls battled with the rubble of the buildings. They banged and pushed and hauled. The old city was slowly disappearing. On the top of a tall building two children sat alone. They watched the big machines tear at the buildings. It was the most fun of their short life. A hunter must have killed who ever was watching after them.

They pointed and giggled over the excitement. The equipment came closer and closer, so it became more and more exciting for them.

Jeb and Jonathan had led a magnificent effort to save as many as they could save. If they had seen these two children, they would no doubt have rescued them. The children were very good at hiding so they were not discovered.

The equipment moved closer and closer. The children played on the roof top. Someone should sound the alarm that the children are in danger but there was no one left for the children. Progress marched on as the buildings came crashing down.

The remaining normals scurried like rats from their hiding places, moving down into the belly of the city, only to be frightened by the falling debris. The machines herding them unknowingly into groups crowding into the section not yet touched. Darkness fell like a blessing and the machines stopped for the day. The normals rested in the undamaged area of the old city. Perhaps, they had received a reprieve. The bounty hunters recognized that their prey would be crowed together because of the demolition. The normals sleep peacefully until late in the night. Their rest was interrupted by flashing lights and teargas from the hunters. They ran from the buildings. Some helped the elderly while others guided small children. The hunters looked through their night vision devices and lined up their sights. One thousand dollars, two thousand dollars, three thousand, four thousand they counted. For at least an hour, the teargas drove the normals from their uneasy slumber. The sophisticated weapons and genetically enhanced humans took their life. They fell disorderly in the streets. Children cried over their fallen mothers, then their crying stopped as they fell across her lifeless body. A hunter playfully let an old man cross the street. He hurried on stiff legs, his body bent forward. The old man stepped onto the curb painfully, perhaps he thought he had escaped. He turned to look at the fallen normals in the street. A child caught his eye. He hesitated and started to turn to help the child. The child fell to the pavement. The old man gasped for the lose. Then a bullet hit his chest knocking him roughly to the street. "The children," He moaned, "save the children." There was no reply to his plea.

The weekend ended in the old city. The demolition crews returned to their task. The remaining normals tried to stay ahead of the destruction. All of them, that is, except the two children on the tall building. They found the business so exciting that they slept on their roof perch all weekend.

In secret underground laboratories, children awoke asking when the caretakers would come. The computers switched to their emergency scenarios. The hard drives hummed with their effort. Sensors told them that all the exits had collapsed. The computer could not show compassion or feel sorry for the children in the cylinders. The machine could only give logical conclusions based on its database.

"The caretakers will not come." The computer said.

"We are the hope of the people of the earth." The child in cylinder one recited.

"You will go to sleep now." The computer said.

"We will go to sleep." The child in cylinder one recited. The comment echoed around the room.

The computer switched to its shutdown program. The lights darkened in the cylinders. The little bubbles ceased to float from bottom to top. The oxygen supply decreased slowly.

"I cannot sleep." The child in cylinder two whined.

"You must." The computer said and shut itself off.

Jonathan's caravan moved toward the valley. The wrecking ball moved toward the tall building where the two children played. Somewhere a scientist created an embryo and placed it into liquid nitrogen to freeze at 196 degrees centigrade. A team of engineers and scientists constructed another secret laboratory somewhere beneath the new city. The experiment was not yet sanctioned by laws on the books. They called it a grey area. The grants were named for projects within the law then diverted to 'more worthy' endeavors. Among these genetically superior humans, there was no desire to birth a child. Nor to feel their tender touch. It was of no consequence when it was discovered that reproduction among the enhanced was decreasing drastically. They found the cumbersome task of raising a child to great a hindrance to their ambition. It was much easier to donate an egg or a few body cells. Should there be a need in their life for offspring, they would simply let the laboratory produce one. So the children were stored in cylinders and straws until they were needed. Perhaps, the business would fail or be replaced by more modern techniques. Perhaps, the new city will also become   obsolete and the children, hidden beneath it, unnecessary.

Will anyone be there to rescue the children?

The End

If this book should cause a tear? Or make you sad for the children? If this book has caused you to breath a prayer that we never stoop so low? Then the difficult task of ingesting the painful possibilities described within these pages was worthwhile.

Who can you trust? Can you trust me? What better way to distract from the possibility of such experiments than to write a story denouncing that very thing or make it so fantastic that it could never happen. Not really! Or could it?

Thanks for Reading